Winters ... for h... ... ...y
has uncovered his scheme. But can she marry off
the eligible executives before Dad sets his
crazy plan in motion?

* * *

"Go home, Sarah."

"No. I think it's time we had this out."

"I don't," Matt said. He couldn't. Good bosses didn't romance their subordinates.

Completely catching him off guard, Sarah marched around his desk and trapped him in his seat by anchoring her hands on both arms of his chair. "I do."

In their entire work association, Matt didn't think they had ever been this close. He could smell the light floral scent of her perfume and see the flecks of gold in her green eyes.

"You should be thanking me, Sarah, for being a gentleman."

"What the heck is that supposed to mean?"

"It means that if we were in any other kind of circumstance, I would be doing this right now." Before she had a chance to react, Matt pulled her into his lap. Then he lowered his head for a kiss.

Dear Reader,

If you're like me, you can't get enough heartwarming love stories and real-life fairy tales that end happily ever after. You'll find what you need and so much more with Silhouette Romance each month.

This month you're in for an extra treat. Bestselling author Susan Meier kicks off MARRYING THE BOSS'S DAUGHTER—the brand-new six-book series written exclusively for Silhouette Romance. In this launch title, *Love, Your Secret Admirer* (#1684), our favorite matchmaking heiress helps a naive secretary snare her boss's attention with an eye-catching makeover.

A sexy rancher discovers love and the son he never knew, when he matches wits with a beautiful teacher, in *What a Woman Should Know* (#1685) by Cara Colter. And a not-so plain Jane captures a royal heart, in *To Kiss a Sheik* (#1686) by Teresa Southwick, the second of three titles in her sultry DESERT BRIDES miniseries.

Debrah Morris brings you a love story of two lifetimes, in *When Lightning Strikes Twice* (#1687), the newest paranormal love story in the SOULMATES series. And sparks sizzle between an innocent curator—with a big secret—and the town's new lawman, in *Ransom* (#1688) by Diane Pershing. Will a seamstress's new beau still love her when he learns she is an undercover heiress? Find out in *The Bridal Chronicles* (#1689) by Lissa Manley.

Be my guest and feed your need for tender and lighthearted romance with all six of this month's great new love stories from Silhouette Romance.

Enjoy!

Mavis C. Allen
Associate Senior Editor, Silhouette Romance

Please address questions and book requests to:
Silhouette Reader Service
U.S.: 3010 Walden Ave., P.O. Box 1325, Buffalo, NY 14269
Canadian: P.O. Box 609, Fort Erie, Ont. L2A 5X3

Love, Your Secret Admirer

SUSAN MEIER

Marrying
The Boss's
Daughter

SILHOUETTE *Romance*®

Published by Silhouette Books

America's Publisher of Contemporary Romance

Special thanks and acknowledgment are given
to Susan Meier for her contribution to the
MARRYING THE BOSS'S DAUGHTER series.

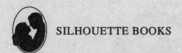 SILHOUETTE BOOKS

ISBN 0-373-19684-9

LOVE, YOUR SECRET ADMIRER

SUSAN MEIER

is one of eleven children, and though she has yet to write a book about a big family, many of her books explore the dynamics of "unusual" family situations, such as large work "families," bosses who behave like overprotective fathers, or "sister" bonds created between friends. Because she has more than twenty nieces and nephews, children also are always popping up in her stories. Many of the funny scenes in her books are based on experiences raising her own children or interacting with her nieces and nephews.

She was born and raised in western Pennsylvania and continues to live in Pennsylvania.

FROM THE DESK OF EMILY WINTERS

Six Bachelor Executives To Go

Bachelor #1: Love, Your Secret Admirer
Matthew Burke—Hmm...his sweet assistant clearly has googly eyes for her workaholic boss. Maybe I can make some office magic happen....

Bachelor #2: Her Pregnant Agenda
Grant Lawson—The guy's a dead ringer for Pierce Brosnan—who wouldn't want to fall into his strong, protective arms!

Bachelor #3: Fill-In Fiancée
Brett Hamilton—The playboy from England has some aristocratic ways about him. Maybe he's royalty and I can find him a princess!

Bachelor #4: Santa Brought a Son
Reed Connors—The ambitious VP seems to have a heavy heart. Who broke it, and where is she now?

Bachelor #5: Rules of Engagement
Nate Leeman—Definitely a lone wolf kind of guy. A bit hard around the edges, but I'll bet there's a tender heart inside.

Bachelor #6: One Bachelor To Go
Jack Devon—The man is so frustratingly elusive. Arrogant and implacable, too, darn it! I'll put him last on my matchmaking list until I can figure out what kind of woman he likes.

Prologue

"We've got a problem."

Carmella Lopez watched as Emily Winters looked up from the report she was reading. Emily's desk was in front of a wall of windows, and the lights of the Boston skyline twinkled behind her, highlighting her brown hair and sapphire-blue eyes. The nighttime view also illustrated that it was long past the hour when most of the employees of Wintersoft, Inc., had gone home. Emily was as intelligent and dedicated as she was beautiful, and that was why Carmella was so annoyed by the conversation she'd overheard Emily's dad having with his sister that afternoon. Emily didn't need to have a man "help" her run her father's company when he retired, any more than she needed help finding a husband.

Emily said, "Spill it."

Carmella stepped into Emily's office and closed the door behind her. She had been Lloyd Winters' executive assistant for twenty-five years, first when he was an investment banker and now at his financial software company. But she also came from a family that had survived being chased out of Mexico several generations ago by Pancho Villa, and she knew that sometimes discretion wasn't the better part of valor. Action was. Though she would never do anything disloyal to Lloyd, she felt a sense of responsibility to his daughter. In a way, acting on her loyalty to Emily protected Lloyd.

"Your dad is about to play matchmaker."

Emily's face lost its color. "Again?"

"I think he's forgotten that he already tried this and failed. This morning, he took one look at our organizational chart and saw that most of our senior vice presidents are eligible bachelors and wheels started turning in his head. I overheard him telling your Aunt Anne in Florida that each of the guys on the chart makes a respectable salary. All of them have proven themselves. And all of them are acceptable son-in-law material."

Emily looked as though she'd faint. "Dear God. Fixing me up with one Wintersoft employee was bad enough," she said, speaking of the disastrous marriage that had resulted when Emily had tried to please her dad by marrying one of Wintersoft's former executives, Todd Baxter. "Marrying me off to everybody who's available will make me a laughingstock."

Carmella softened her tone because, in spite of his sometimes overbearing, old-fashioned tactics, Lloyd's heart was always in the right place. "He doesn't mean it that way."

"He didn't mean it that way the last time, either. But that's exactly what happened. The tension was so thick when my marriage to Todd collapsed that Todd had to leave the company, and I lost credibility with most of the staff. It's taken me five years of working nearly nonstop to prove myself again."

''But you did it. And earned a senior vice presidency in the process. Plus, the five years it took you to be promoted proved you didn't just get your job because you're Lloyd Winters' daughter. No one can say that you don't deserve your position.''

''No, but they can lose respect for me. Who's going to take seriously a woman whose dad is trying to auction her off to the highest-ranking corporate officer?'' Emily raked her fingers through her thick, shoulder-length hair. ''I'm going to have to quit.''

Carmella shook her head. ''You can't quit. That would mean explaining to your dad why you were leaving and it would kill him to think he pushed you away. He's not trying to push you away; he's trying to help you. It might be old-fashioned, but I'm guessing your dad believes marrying you off to one of the senior vice presidents—someone who could take over the company when he retires instead of you—is a way to give you options. If you don't have to replace him, you would be free to be a wife and a mother—if that was what you wanted.''

''I don't know what I want. Maybe I do want to be a wife and mother one day, but that's my decision. I just need time.'' Emily drew a frustrated breath. ''Things would be so much easier if my dad and I could talk about this. But since the mess with Todd, it's like we don't even speak the same language anymore.''

''Talking won't help. Once your dad gets an idea in his head, it's impossible to get it out. He has hundreds of reasons to want to see you married and a mother. You would have to have a hundred arguments to change his mind.''

Emily groaned. ''I'm doomed!''

''Not really. Not if we think of something to distract

him before he starts hooking you up with his senior VPs, or if we come up with a way that makes it impossible for him to play matchmaker.''

"We could just marry off everybody who's single before my dad gets to them," Emily said flippantly.

Carmella laughed. "Now, that would be something," she said, but she paused. "Actually, that *would* be something."

"Oh, no!" Emily said. "Don't you start! This isn't like *Seven Brides for Seven Brothers!*"

"You're right. I don't think we have that many matches to make." Carmella rushed around Emily's desk and reached into the top desk drawer for a copy of the organizational chart. The first block listed Emily's dad, Lloyd Winters, as CEO and President of Wintersoft, Inc. Nine lines led from that box to the next row of blocks holding the names of the senior vice presidents. Listed below each of them were the names of their staff members.

For the present, Carmella concentrated on the senior vice presidents themselves. "Alan Richards and Chad Evers are already married."

Carmella watched Emily's eyes widen as she apparently considered being paired up with either of the fortyish, balding dads, and she laughed. "Dodged a bullet on those two, didn't you?"

"Very funny."

"Okay," Carmella continued, once again pointing to the chart. "Melinda McIntosh, Senior Vice President of Human Resources, is female. So she, Chad and Alan are out. That leaves these five. Matt Burke, Grant Lawson, Brett Hamilton, Nate Leeman, and Jack Devon." She pointed to one more block. "Reed Connors is only a vice president, but I'm pretty sure he's about to be promoted to senior vice president, and he's single. So I don't think we should leave him out.''

Emily stared at the chart. ''I can see why my dad's striking now. The iron is definitely hot. Except for Jack Devon who's so elusive even I wouldn't know where to start with him, any one of these other guys is ripe for the picking.''

''Which means we have our work cut out for us.''

Emily peered at Carmella. ''I can't see how our marrying off six unsuspecting men is any different than my dad marrying me off.''

''It's very different,'' Carmella assured her. ''Because we would be smart and careful. We wouldn't just pair these men up with women willy-nilly. We would approach it like a business problem.''

Thinking that through, Emily sat back in her seat. ''Okay. If we handled this the same way we would any business undertaking, we would have to work in earnest to find the right mates for these guys.''

Carmella smiled. ''Yes, we would.''

''We would have to be fair, and look out for the best interests of all parties involved.''

''There's no other way to do this.''

Emily tapped her pencil on her desk blotter. ''The only problem is, a plan like this would take lots of time and we might not have lots of time.''

''We can buy a few weeks by having you pretend to be dating someone.''

''If I could just pick a boyfriend off a boyfriend tree, I wouldn't be in this predicament right now.''

''You could ask Steven Hansen to help us out.''

''Steven? But he's…''

''From New York City,'' Carmella said, stopping Emily before she said what she was about to say because in this case it was irrelevant. Getting them back to the real matter at hand, she added, "I can find most of the background on our guys on the Internet, so we wouldn't even have to leave the building to do what we need to do."

Carmella paused and frowned thoughtfully before adding, "But convincing your dad you're dating Steven probably won't last beyond the charity ball at the end of the month, so I suggest we go for the obvious one first." She pointed at a name on the organizational chart.

Emily smiled broadly. "Oh, my gosh! That's perfect."

Chapter One

Timing is everything.

Sarah Morris, the executive assistant to the Senior Vice President of Accounting for Wintersoft, looked up from her work when Penny Rutledge, Wintersoft's petite blond receptionist, set a huge crystal vase containing one dozen long-stemmed white roses on her desk.

"Oh, my! They're beautiful!"

"Open the card," Penny said shifting from foot to foot, dancing with excitement.

Sarah pushed her glasses up the bridge of her nose, then fingered the practical braid she'd woven her waist-length red hair into as she peered down at her ordinary gray suit. "They're for me?"

"Of course they're for you, silly! Open the card."

The scent of roses filled the air as Sarah fumbled with the envelope. The seal finally gave and she pulled out the brightly colored rectangle and read out loud, "Your Secret Admirer."

Penny all but swooned. "Ohh!"

"I have a secret admirer?" Sarah said, her voice confused and uncertain. She had moved from North Dakota to Boston a year ago, but didn't get out much. The only man she knew more than casually was...

An amazing thought occurred to her and she glanced over her shoulder to the office behind her. Her boss, Matt Burke, sat at his desk, making his to-do list for the next workday because that's what he did *every* day at five minutes till five. Fridays were no exception.

He diligently scribbled in his calendar, oblivious to her scrutiny, but Sarah drank in every detail of his short, spiky brown hair and handsome face. Because he was writing, she couldn't see his eyes but knew they were a soft blue, trimmed with unusually long black lashes. More than once she had dreamily gazed into them when he was focused on something else.

It couldn't be...

Matt wouldn't...

"So who do you think it is?" Penny asked as she happily rearranged the flowers to make the bouquet perfect.

"I don't know," Sarah said, trying not to look behind her again. Working one-on-one the way she and Matt did, they knew enough intimate details of each other's lives to throw them into the category of friends. But Matt had never shown one ounce of interest in her as a woman.

"No idea at all?" Penny said, smiling as she leaned a hip against Sarah's desk and got comfortable. "No guy you met at a bar or museum or church on Sunday morning?"

"I don't go to bars. People don't usually strike up conversations with me at museums and they are even quieter in church." Which made it highly unlikely that she would have a secret admirer. And that took her back to Matt. He was the only man who could have sent her these flowers. The question was…why?

"I heard you got roses!" Carmella Lopez said as she walked down the open corridor to Sarah's workstation. Lloyd Winters' executive assistant was a beautiful Hispanic woman with short, graying black hair and warm brown eyes. A fifty-something widow with no children, Carmella was also a sweet and sincere office mother hen who read romance novels. It didn't surprise Sarah that she would be one of the first people in the office to congratulate a woman who got flowers. "Who are they from?"

Sarah glanced at Carmella. "A secret admirer."

Matt stepped out of his office, and, as always, Sarah's attention was immediately consumed by him. Tall and broad-shouldered, ruggedly attractive even in his dress shirt and tie, he looked more like one of the employees on Sarah's dad's ranch than a quiet, focused senior vice president for a software company. Sarah suspected that was why she had such a crush on him. In her mind, he combined the best of both worlds. He had the masculinity of a cowboy and the brains and conceptualizing ability of a Forbes, Ford or Gates.

His gaze flitted to the roses then swung to hers. "Well, look at this," he said, his voice filled with that odd tone men used when they tried to be happy about something girlie, but didn't quite know how to pull it off. Or, when they were in some way faking their response. "Somebody sent you flowers."

It was him! Sarah thought, tamping down the unrealistic hope that he'd sent her flowers because he was interested in her. The tone of his voice was too patronizing and too brotherly. If he'd sent them, it was to cheer her up. Or—she squeezed her eyes shut then quickly opened them again before anyone noticed—because he felt sorry for her. He knew she didn't go out on weekends. He knew she hadn't had a date since she'd arrived in Boston.

"Yes, and aren't they beautiful?" Carmella fingered a pristine petal. "White is for what?"

"Purity," Sarah replied, her eyes narrowing. Purity? *Purity!*

"So some man thinks you're very sweet," Matt said, smiling his warm, wonderful, I'm-a-friendly-guy smile and Sarah wanted to deck him. The man she was crazy about thought she was *pure*. While she daydreamed about his kisses, he saw her as someone inexperienced and naive.

For fifty cents she'd take him to her dad's ranch where she played poker with the hands and held her own during cattle drives when the cursing was thick and biting. She would show him firsthand that she wasn't naive, she wasn't inexperienced and she sure as hell wasn't pure.

"Well, you can't leave them here," Carmella was saying as Sarah forced herself out of her reverie. "They'll die over the weekend." She smiled at Sarah. "Besides don't you want to enjoy them?"

"No," Sarah said, surprising herself as much as everybody else around her. "I don't want to enjoy them, because I don't want them at all. Penny, you can have them."

"No!"

"No!"

"No!"

Matt, Penny and Carmella said the word simultaneously. Penny said it like a woman who didn't want the flowers of another woman, no matter how lovely.

Carmella sounded shocked that Sarah would give away such beauty. Matt said it as if she had suggested prematurely withdrawing money from her IRA.

The red numbers on Sarah's digital clock blinked and 4:59 became 5:00. Sarah opened her bottom desk drawer, withdrew her backpack and rose from her seat. "Then leave them for the cleaning people," she said as she left her office.

Tears stung her eyes. Her gray skirt shifted across her calves. Her fat braid bounced along her back. Damn it! She *was* pure. Well, not exactly pure, more like conservative. Well, not even conservative, more like comfortable. She had thick unruly hair that fell to the bottom of her back, so it wasn't just convenient to wear it in a braid. It was comfortable. Her glasses were less effort than her contacts. And long skirts were all-covering, easy to match and the most logical thing to wear when she was constantly bending and stretching to reach files.

She was dowdy, and conservative by virtue of the fact that she dressed for comfort, and there was no way she would have a secret admirer. She hadn't even had a date since she'd set foot in this city! Combining her lack of dates with her dowdy clothes, Matt probably saw her as some kind of charity case. Did he know she was still a virgin, too?

Purity flowers took on a whole new meaning, sending anger careening through Sarah's veins. The probability that Matt had sent those flowers because he felt sorry for her became more and more obvious by the second. By the time she reached the elevator, she just wanted to die.

Matt Burke stood with Carmella and Penny, watching Sarah as she marched, head high, to the elevator. His thoughts were in such turmoil and the situation was so unusual—not to mention uncomfortable—that he wasn't sure what to do.

"Go after her."

Matt faced Carmella. "What?"

"Go after her. She can't leave these beautiful flowers."

Matt almost said, "Yes, she can," but he changed his mind. He wasn't sure why seeing Sarah get flowers caused a tightening in his chest, he only knew it did. Now that he'd gotten over the shock that Sarah would waste perfectly good roses, he wasn't upset to see her leave them behind. In fact, he had an ungodly urge to toss them out his office window.

"I'll take them to her," Penny said, grabbing the flowers and pivoting toward the door.

"No!" Carmella yelped as she caught Penny's hand, but she lowered her voice and said, "Matt will take them to her." She paused to lift the vase from Penny's grasp, and her smile reappeared as she offered the roses to Matt. "You drive by her apartment complex on your way home. You can take them right to her door."

"Oh, no!" Matt said, backing away from the flowers as if they were poisonous. "She doesn't want these."

Carmella chuckled. "So what? If she refuses to take them from you, the worst that could happen is that you'd get stuck with a dozen long-stemmed roses and a beautiful vase."

Penny said, "Maybe he's afraid someone will mistake him for a delivery man."

Matt sighed heavily. "I'm not afraid of anything! I just know she doesn't want them. I'll feel like an idiot going to her door with flowers that she doesn't want."

Carmella sauntered around Sarah's desk and picked up the card. "I don't think she ran because she *didn't* want the flowers."

Matt said, "Huh?"

"I think she ran because she *did* want the flowers."

"Ohhhh!" Penny said. "I get it. When I set the roses on her desk she was excited. When she saw the card, she got mad. It's like she wants flowers from somebody, but she doesn't know who sent these."

Carmella nodded. "So she doesn't know if her secret admirer is the man she wants it to be. And if it *is* the man she wants it to be, she's probably angry that he wasn't mature enough to sign his name."

"You guys are nuts," Matt said, though their rationale did make an odd kind of sense. Sarah might be too calm and pragmatic to behave like a swooning female. But if there was somebody she liked, somebody she really, really liked and she wanted to get flowers from him, Matt could see Sarah getting angry that the guy was too chicken to sign his name.

In Matt's opinion, Sarah was much too good for this coward.

Penny reverently whispered, "She must really like him."

Carmella only smiled.

Matt felt as though somebody had punched him in the stomach. He couldn't believe that Sarah had fallen for somebody and that he hadn't noticed. He couldn't believe the man she'd fallen for was a spineless idiot who didn't know how to make a decent move. A move that involved admitting who he was. He couldn't believe Sarah falling for someone bothered him more than the fact that the guy was a spineless idiot. But he did know it probably wasn't wise for him to be the person going to her apartment right now.

"A woman should do this."

"I have a salon appointment," Carmella said. "Penny lives across town. Besides, she has kids to go home to."

"I can't take these to her!"

"Why not?"

"Because I'm not that sensitive. I don't know what to say. I don't know how to get her to accept these flowers." And he wasn't even sure he wanted to. That was the tricky part.

Carmella sighed. "Matt, what day is it?"

"August 29."

"What's Monday?"

"September 1."

"What happens on September 1?"

"It's Labor Day, but on Tuesday my staff goes to work on the quarterly report."

Carmella handed him the vase of roses. "A wise man who had a quarterly report due would want his executive assistant at her desk on Tuesday morning. Sarah looked pretty mad when she left. You don't want her to spend her long weekend brooding and be too tired or too upset to come in."

Matt groaned.

"Take these flowers to her, make her understand that it doesn't matter who sent them. What matters is that somebody cares about her."

Matt shook his head, as affronted as Sarah. "Then why couldn't he sign his name?"

Carmella shrugged. "Haven't you ever been so tongue-tied with someone that you watched from a distance because you couldn't go up to her and talk?"

Matt swallowed. He did know what it was like to be so tongue-tied with someone that he watched her from a distance rather than make real contact. It wasn't a lover or potential lover. It was his mother. And he had been ten at the time.

"Think of this guy like that. Somebody who is inexperienced or somebody who likes Sarah so much that he's afraid to make a mistake."

Matt stared at the flowers. His situation wasn't anything like the situation Carmella was describing, but she had struck the right nerve. The feeling was the same. He'd never approached his mother back then because the fear of rejection was stronger than the hope that she'd welcome him with open arms. He knew this flower-sender's emotions like the back of his hand.

"When you give the flowers to Sarah explain that somebody who doesn't know how to admit it likes her and she should be flattered."

"And you think that will cheer her up?"

Carmella and Penny simultaneously said, "Yes."

"Fine," Matt said, turning to go into his office for his briefcase. "Get me her address."

Forty minutes later Sarah opened her apartment door and there stood her boss, holding the purity flowers he had sent her because he felt sorry for her. Heat scalded her cheeks as her blood pressure and anger rose.

"Hi."

She drew a long breath, not sure what to say that wouldn't contain a curse word. Pure. Ha! If he pushed her she would show him pure.

"Carmella was right. You can't just leave these at the office over the weekend."

"Sure I can."

"Well, it's physically possible," Matt agreed, "but it's not right."

"Sure it is."

"No, it's not. Let me in so I can explain these flowers to you."

For three seconds Sarah only stared at him, blown away by his very casual admission that he had sent the roses. How else would he be able to explain them?

Too curious to hear what he had to say to reject him out of hand, she said, "All right. Come in."

Sarah saw him glance around as if trying to waste some time before delving into the explanation he probably suspected would get him punched. As he looked at the solid khaki sofa and chair, accented by fat floral pillows and thick wood end tables with brass lamps, she didn't say a word.

He set the roses on her coffee table. "I figured out why you're mad about these."

She tossed her head and crossed her arms beneath her breasts, shifting her braid over her shoulder and bunching the bulky material of her skirt at her waist. She felt like Mother Hubbard. "Did you?"

"Yes. You're upset that someone can like you but be too cowardly to sign his name to a card when he sends you flowers."

Though that wasn't it at all, Sarah considered his explanation. At the core of it was an admission that he liked her. Of course, he could be saying that he liked her as a friend, but if that was all it was, he could have signed his name.

"What else?"

Matt shook his head. "What do you mean? What else?"

"You're the expert here. I'm just the person who got the flowers."

"I'm not sure I'm an expert, but I do understand this guy's feelings." He caught her gaze. "Haven't you ever liked somebody enough that you stood across the street and stared at their house, too afraid to approach them?"

"I grew up on a ranch."

"Okay, have you ever called somebody and then hung up when they answered?"

"Not since caller I.D."

"You're not helping, Sarah!"

"I don't want to help you. I want to understand."

Matt sighed. "I'm not sure I understand it myself."

"Well, if you don't understand," Sarah shouted, angry again. "How the hell am I supposed to understand?"

Matt's face lit with enthusiasm. "Now, see, there's one thing right there. Saying hell isn't such a big deal, but it reminds me that you grew up with a bunch of men, and when you get angry you can curse better than most of my friends."

"And that's a reason to send me *purity* flowers?"

"Maybe the person who sent the flowers sees there's another side to you?"

Because Matt was still talking about the flower sender as if he were a third party, Sarah realized that there had to be an explanation for why he couldn't talk about this directly. She fell to her sofa in exhaustion, and decided that for now, going along would be the easiest thing to do.

"I'm confused. He doesn't like my cursing so he sent me flowers to let me know he thinks I'm pure?"

"No, he sent you flowers because he's telling you

that he sees something about you that nobody else sees.''

''Why not just tell me with words?''

''Maybe he's shy.''

Sarah narrowed her eyes at Matt. ''Shy?''

''All right, you don't like shy,'' Matt said, clearly exasperated, further confirming that he hated talking about this directly. ''How about this? To have your name and business address, this guy has to be somebody you know. Probably somebody you work with.'' He caught her gaze. ''That means there's a relationship of some sort already in place that he doesn't want to lose. So, he's not going to make a move until he sees how you and everybody at Wintersoft react to these flowers.''

Dumbfounded, Sarah only stared at Matt, realizing she should have thought of this herself. Cautious Matt would never get involved with a woman he feared might reject him. Especially not someone he worked with. There was no way he'd jeopardize their good boss/assistant relationship, particularly since he would also be risking the embarrassment of being snubbed in front of the entire staff of Wintersoft.

''So, what am I supposed to do?''

''You can't control the reactions of everybody at Wintersoft, but you could at least send this guy the message that you're interested in him too.''

''I can't just tell him?''

''You don't know who he is, remember?''

Sarah squeezed her eyes shut, focusing herself on the project as he wanted it because he was calling the shots. ''Right. So what do I do?''

''Well, he sent you flowers to let you know he's interested. You have to send him a signal that you're interested.''

''Send him a signal?''

''Yeah, you know,'' Matt said, motioning with his hand. ''Dress up or something.''

Sarah frowned. ''Dress up? Are you saying I don't dress right?''

Matt shook his head. ''No. You dress fine for the office. But what you wear to the office isn't going to tell a guy you're interested.''

''So I need to dress prettier?''

''More like feminine. You're an attractive girl, Sarah. But you hide that. In the office, that's not a big deal because you're supposed to be focused on work not the way you look. But if you want to show a guy you're interested, the short route would be to bring out your feminine side.''

''My feminine side,'' Sarah repeated, staring into Matt's beautiful blue eyes. She was flooded with something soft and warm, yet also exciting. He wanted her to bring out her feminine side—which meant he saw she had a feminine side and might even have daydreamed about that part of her the way she'd daydreamed about his kisses.

Suddenly feeling female and desirable, she removed her glasses and smiled demurely at Matt.

And Matt's heart flip-flopped. He had always seen the pretty face behind the glasses, and, just like her secret admirer, Matt knew there was another side to her, a more feminine side. But unlike her secret admirer, he couldn't do a darned thing about it.

He rose from her sofa. ''So, you understand about the flowers then?''

She nodded. ''Yeah. I get it.''

"Good," Matt said, walking to her door. He tried to tell himself that he wasn't upset that she was about to get involved with someone, but he was. Unfortunately, he also knew that as her immediate supervisor, he wasn't allowed to be attracted to her, so he would have to get over it. And he would. With a quarterly statement that had to be done before October fifteenth, he couldn't let disappointment over a woman divert his attention.

He grabbed the doorknob, but didn't open the door. Instead, he faced her. "And I'll see you Tuesday?"

"Yes," she said, smiling again.

Looking at her beautiful smile and her pretty green eyes, Matt's heart jerked to double time. He had an almost irresistible urge to kiss her, or at the very least ask her out. After an entire year of being good friends, suddenly he felt entitled to be the guy who got to know the other woman he knew she was hiding in there.

But he couldn't. She was his assistant. And if that wasn't enough to keep him in line, he also had a life plan. It didn't exactly prevent him from dating, but it did preclude him from doing anything that messed up his source of income and his career. He needed his salary and bonuses to fund the investments he had chosen to reach his goal of being a multimillionaire before he was forty. Forty was young enough that he would still have plenty of time to get married and have children. Plus, that gave him nine more years to fund his investments, which—because he was a savvy speculator—were earning interest and dividends and growing on their own. Everything was going according to plan, so now was not the time to turn into a risk taker. Dating his executive assistant was definitely a risk.

Besides, after she sent the message to her secret admirer that she was interested, she would be dating somebody else.

Matt left Sarah's apartment and she all but danced for joy. She couldn't believe it! He liked her! He'd sent her flowers, explained why when she misinterpreted them and then told her how to respond.

She paused in her dancing.

Dear God. All Matt had really told her was that he wanted her to be more feminine.

Though Sarah knew she cleaned up well and also knew she could easily never swear again, she had to admit she wasn't in touch with that other side of herself Matt claimed to see. And that was the part he liked. If she wanted to prove to him that their office romance could work, she not only had to uncover the part of her that he liked, she really had to become that woman.

Realizing this was beyond her, she fell to her sofa trying to think of someone who could help her. Two of her Wintersoft coworkers, Ariana Fitzpatrick and Sunny Robbins, immediately came to mind, but she discounted both because Ariana was pregnant and Sunny was busy with law school. Sarah didn't want to impose on either of them. Especially not on a Friday night when both were probably up to their ears in well-deserved bubble baths!

Besides, what she needed was the help of someone who truly understood men and woman and romance.

Men, women and *romance?*

A thought struck her and she reached for her portable phone and the little book of telephone numbers on her end table.

No one knew more about romance than Carmella Lopez.

Chapter Two

After a long Labor Day weekend of visiting salons, shopping and long discussions over choices at the makeup counter, Sarah sat on the fat khaki chair in her living room across from Carmella Lopez and Emily Winters, daughter of Lloyd Winters, owner of Wintersoft.

When Sarah had called Carmella Friday night, Carmella had suggested they enlist Emily's help with Sarah's makeover because Emily bridged the gap between Carmella's and Sarah's generations. And she had been correct. Using bits and pieces of the experience of three females of varying ages, they had turned Sarah into a stunning woman. With a closet full of new clothes, a new hairdo and just the right makeup, she now had as much confidence about her looks as she had about roping cattle.

"So, are you nervous about tomorrow?" Carmella asked, setting her teacup on the wooden coffee table, right beside the vase of white roses that had started all this.

Sarah looked lovingly at the white blooms. "Surprisingly, no. I know I asked for your help as part of a plan to show Matt I could be feminine, but something else happened. I feel like I've finally found the real me."

"Finding the real you is actually the point of a makeover," Carmella said with a short laugh.

"And simple and sensual is definitely you," Emily agreed. A satisfied smile curved her lips, and her sapphire-blue eyes sparkled with approval. "You look great."

"I feel great. I feel confident enough to conquer the world."

Carmella frowned. "I hope this doesn't mean you've changed your mind about Matt!"

"No!" Sarah said. "I really like Matt. If he's interested in me, I want a chance with him, too."

"Well, if he doesn't get that message from your new look, then he's blind," Carmella said, rising from the sofa.

"Right," Emily agreed as she also rose. "We'll see you tomorrow. Remember, come to work a half hour early. The weather report says rain, so you may want some time to pull yourself together before you make the walk down the hall to your office."

Already at the door, Carmella asked, "Are you sure you're not uncomfortable making an entrance?"

Sarah laughed. "I think it's what I need to do. Go for the shock value, get my new self out in the open right off the bat and see how he reacts."

"I think so, too," Carmella said and squeezed Sarah's hands. "We'll see you tomorrow."

Sarah let her new friends out of her apartment, then

closed the door behind them, wondering if she would get any sleep. She wasn't nervous about seeing Matt. But she did know he might not react the way Emily and Carmella believed he would because she hadn't exactly done as he had asked her to do.

For the first time since she'd received the flowers, she was glad for the secret admirer cover. Just as Matt had used it to get his point across to her, Sarah planned to use it to get her point across to him. Looking for her femininity had brought out a sexy side of her personality that even Sarah hadn't known she had. But when she considered her natural boldness, she knew being confident about her sexuality was her true personality, a part of who she was, and she couldn't change that. If Matt didn't want her as she really was, it would break her heart, but at least they would have the cover of anonymity so no one besides Carmella and Emily would know the exchange had occurred.

Matt looked up from his desk Monday morning and the sight that greeted him caused his breath to catch and his mouth to fall open in awe. Sarah walked up the aisle to her workstation, her head high, a smile on her lips.

Her long red hair had been cut and her braid had been replaced by a hairdo that could only be described as sensual. Fat locks of looping curls cascaded to her shoulders and bounced with every step she took.

Her cinnamon-colored suit looked like suede. The skirt was short and Matt could see enough of her legs to realize she hadn't been hiding just a feminine woman beneath the bland skirts and jackets she usually wore. She had been hiding a goddess.

He rose from his seat and cautiously made his way to the workspace she shared with Sunny Robbins.

"Sarah?"

"Oh, good morning, Matt."

She greeted him as if there was nothing different about her appearance today, and for ten seconds Matt couldn't decide if he should say something or let it alone. He knew he had been the one to tell her to change the way she dressed, but he hadn't expected she would turn into a completely different person, and he wasn't sure his real reaction to her new look would be appropriate. What he wanted to do was whistle.

She bent to toss her little brown purse into her desk drawer and Matt's gaze traveled the curve created by her shapely derriere, down the long length of leg to brown high heels of stiletto proportions and he felt as if his heart stopped. His common sense, boss instincts and attraction all got jumbled and before he knew what was happening, he gasped, "What did you do to yourself?"

Sarah straightened quickly, a stricken look on her face. "You don't like it?"

"Like it? Dear God. You're going to give half the men on staff coronaries."

Her face brightened. Her well-painted lips curved into a smile. "So, I did okay?"

"Okay? Sarah, you look like a totally different person."

Her stricken expression returned. "I hope you mean that in a good way." She paused and bit her bottom lip. "Because this is the real me." She caught his gaze. "And I want my secret admirer to see the real me."

The quivering that had set up residence in Matt's abdomen turned to a rock of misery. He might have been the one to instruct Sarah to change a bit for her secret admirer, but, at the time, the guy had seemed more theory than a real person. With that comment, Sarah turned Matt's "theory" into a living, breathing male. No longer a concept, but competition. "You did this for your secret admirer?"

"You said I needed to be more feminine."

"I said feminine," Matt argued, not because he didn't like her look, but because he did. He *really* did. But he couldn't have her. Some other guy would be the recipient of all this femininity. "I didn't say…"

"Sexy?" Sarah said, interrupting him. Her enthusiasm returned and she smiled broadly. "That was my idea."

"Why?"

Sarah walked around her desk and stood directly in front of him. "Because after talking to Carmella and Emily on Friday night, I realized that feminine for me would be sexy."

Matt's brow furrowed. "Carmella Lopez and Emily Winters?"

"Yes. After our discussion about the roses I decided I needed some help with my makeover, I called Carmella and she brought Emily. But we didn't run to a store the minute they arrived at my apartment. We talked first, and they told me that feminine could mean a lot of things."

Not at all willing to hand over *this* Sarah to another man, Matt said, "Yeah, like flowered dresses, little white purses and lace-trimmed gloves."

"I'm sure there are proper ladies in the South who would agree with you." She took a step closer and smiled the smile that made Matt's knees weak. "But I'm not like one of those ladies and I believe my secret admirer needs to see the real me."

"And this is the real you?"

Holding his gaze, she nodded.

Matt stifled the urge to tug at his shirt collar because with her standing about a foot in front of him, smiling her confident, positive, sexy smile, the room was suddenly very warm. "You're sure?"

She nodded again. "Carmella says it's all about confidence and this is the most confident I've felt in years. If I were in a dainty dress with little white gloves I would feel like a fake."

She shifted away from Matt so she could hit the switch to turn on her computer monitor and Matt took the opportunity to loosen his collar so he could catch his breath.

"But the plain suits weren't me, either," she continued. "So we experimented with a few looks until we got to this one and, voilà," she said, facing him again. "Suddenly I felt like me."

"Holy cow!" Sunny Robbins, paralegal to Grant Lawson, Wintersoft's in-house counsel entered the office. Her chin-length sun-kissed brown hair had been tossed about by the September breeze and her black pantsuit was rain-splattered.

Matt quickly glanced back at Sarah. She hadn't worn a coat or a rain hat. Yet her suit was dry and her hair was perfect.

Sunny stopped beside Sarah and ran her gaze from the top of her head to the tips of her perfectly dry, brown, high-heeled sandals.

"Holy cow!"

Sarah laughed. "Thanks. I think."

"Oh, my 'holy cow' definitely deserved a thanks," Sunny said as she rounded Sarah's desk and tossed her purse onto her chair. "You look great."

"I feel great! I feel terrific!"

Sunny laughed. "I would feel terrific, too, if I looked like that! What brought this on?"

Matt glanced at dry, perfectly coifed Sarah again. Something was wrong here. There was no way she got from the bus to this building without getting wet. She must have stopped somewhere and fixed herself up before stepping into the office. If he didn't know better, Matt might think she had actually made an entrance.

His voice slow and cautious, Matt said, "Sarah has a secret admirer."

Both of Sunny's eyebrows rose. "Really?"

"Yeah, he sent me flowers late Friday afternoon," Sarah said. Hearing the odd tone in Matt's voice, she glanced at him, saw the confused expression on his face and decided that look was the final nail in the coffin. From the second she'd arrived, he'd been sputtering and arguing with her choices. Now his quiet voice and unhappy expression confirmed what she'd guessed all along. He didn't like her new look.

The thought made her stomach churn and her knees shake like two leaves in the wind. Worse, her breath wanted to come out in quick panting gasps, but just as Carmella had taught her over the weekend, Sarah controlled all that. Because, deep down inside, she genuinely believed what she had told Matt. This was the real Sarah Morris. If Matt didn't like the real her then she had to move on, find a guy who would like her, exactly as she was. No matter how much it hurt that it wasn't Matt.

"I left the flowers here, Matt brought them to my apartment and we got to talking about why someone would send me flowers anonymously," Sarah said, watching as Matt disappeared into his office. "Matt guessed that the guy wanted some kind of signal from me that I was interested in dating, and this is what Carmella, Emily and I came up with.''

Sunny shot her a skeptical look. ''Matt told you that changing your look would signal the secret admirer to ask you out?''

''Yeah.''

Sunny laughed. ''Just goes to show what he knows! The truth is, Sarah, secret admirers are usually friends trying to cheer you up.''

Sarah frowned. She had thought exactly that. Right from the beginning she'd decided that if Matt had sent her those flowers it was to boost her morale.

''But in your case, I think Matt took advantage of the flowers to go one step further.''

''What do you mean?''

''Well,'' she said, pointing at Sarah. ''Look at you. You look wonderful. One of your friends might have sent you the flowers, but Matt used them to get you to come out of your shell. Lots of guys are going to ask you out. He did you a huge favor.''

With every sentence Sunny spoke, tears pricked Sarah's eyes. She finally understood. She still believed Matt had sent her the flowers, but she now knew he hadn't done it so she would bring out her feminine side for him. It was of no consequence whether or not he liked her new look. He'd encouraged her makeover so she'd find another man.

She'd thought she and Matt were using the secret flower sender facade to protect Matt, but the truth was he might have created the secure forum of a secret admirer for her. That anonymity was the only thing keeping her from dying of embarrassment right now.

But it wasn't doing a darned thing to protect her

bruised heart. He'd never wanted her. He probably hadn't even considered wanting her.

Matt drove to his father's house that evening feeling as if someone had punched him. He'd spent the day watching out his office door as every woman and probably fifty percent of the men employed by Wintersoft had trickled into Sarah's office to see her new "look." All the women had gasped with envy. All the guys had gasped in awe. The single men had asked her out. And Matt's teeth were now ground down to about half their size.

He pulled his SUV into his dad's driveway and climbed out, not sure it was a good idea to keep his long-standing every-other-night dinner date with his dad. He knew he wasn't going to be good company. Worse, he knew his dad would demand to know why.

He didn't even get the whole way up the walk before his dad, Wayne Burke, also a CPA and probably the picture of what Matt would look like at age fifty-five, with his short brown hair, broad shoulders and blue eyes, opened the door.

"Somebody stole your fire truck," he said, referring to the fact that when Matt was seven a neighbor kid had run off with his toy and wouldn't return it until Matt's dad had interfered.

"No," Matt said, as he stepped inside the neat-as-a-pin foyer of the Cape Cod house, not in the mood to play this silly game with his dad.

"Just give me the name and I'll go talk to his father, get it back for you."

"This isn't funny tonight, Dad."

"I think it is. I think it's hysterical," Wayne said and laughed heartily to prove it. "I love it when you're in a bad mood. Gives me a reason to poke into your personal life since you're usually not too free with information. Here, give me your raincoat.''

Though he tried to smile and look like his usual happy-go-lucky self, the raincoat reminded Matt of seeing bone-dry Sarah walk into the office and sent his blood pressure soaring again. He could only figure that Sarah had made an entrance this morning. Given that he and Grant Lawson, Wintersoft's legal counsel, were the only two men in that section of the office, that had to mean Sarah believed Grant had sent her those flowers, and she wanted to look picture-perfect the first time he saw her new look.

But the more Matt thought about it, the more he decided that Sarah would have to know that men like tall, handsome, suave Grant didn't need to send women flowers anonymously. They were bold enough to come right out and say whatever they wanted whenever they wanted. They didn't need to be secret admirers.

Grant himself backed up Matt's theory. If Grant had been the person to send Sarah flowers Friday afternoon, he would have been eager to see her reaction—which in this case was an eye-popping makeover—and he would have commented. Instead, he didn't seem to notice Sarah's makeover when he arrived, and he had stayed sequestered in his office most of the day.

But Matt's whole hypothesis had fallen through when Wintersoft's general counsel had stepped into Sarah and Sunny's workstation two minutes after Sunny had left and started making small talk with Sarah.

Small talk! Lawyers never made small talk. Every word they spoke had a purpose. And, in this case, the only purpose could be that Grant was putting the moves on Sarah.

Matt wanted to punch him.

Wayne closed the closet door and headed for his bright yellow kitchen. "I made your favorite. Roast beef and mashed potatoes."

Matt followed his dad down the hall. "I'm not hungry," he said, then wished he could bite his tongue.

His dad stopped, faced Matt and shook his head. "You know I'm going to get this out of you before the end of the night."

Matt sighed. "There's nothing to get out."

"Great, then I'm sure you'll want seconds on potatoes."

"All right," Matt said, realizing he wasn't in the mood for two hours of twenty questions while being forced to eat mass quantities of food that would taste like sawdust, so he might as well tell the truth and get it over with. "If you have to know, I'm preoccupied because Sarah has a secret admirer."

"Your assistant Sarah?" Wayne asked, pushing open the swinging door that led to his kitchen. The round oak table had been set for dinner.

Matt walked to the refrigerator and grabbed two beers. "Yes."

Wayne laughed. "And you're jealous."

"No. I'm concerned because I think it's Wintersoft's legal counsel, Grant Lawson."

Matt's dad thought for a second before he said, "I must not know him."

"He's a nice enough guy," Matt said, taking his usual seat and setting his napkin on his lap. "But he's divorced and I get the impression he's soured on marriage enough that he'll never take the plunge again."

"Oh, so you're *worried* about Sarah?"

"Yes," Matt said, sighing with relief that his dad

understood. He wasn't jealous. Really. He was *concerned.*

"And you're not even a little jealous?"

"No. Just very concerned," Matt said, but a picture of Sarah in her cinnamon-colored suede suit popped into his head and his chest tightened.

"That's why your face just turned beet-red. Because you're not jealous."

Matt tossed his napkin to the table. "I don't know why I come here to have dinner with you."

"You come here because I'm your dad and I don't let you get away with lying. Especially not to yourself." Wayne served himself a thick slice of pot roast. "Which means you want me to be honest, so I have to come right out and say this. You've got the look of a jealous man on your face."

Matt sighed. "Okay, you want me to come clean. I'll come clean. Sarah got flowers Friday night and, yeah, I got a twinge of jealousy. But I squelched it because bosses are not supposed to date the women they supervise."

Wayne took a big bite of mashed potato, chewed, then said, "So get her transferred."

Matt gaped at his dad. "That would be idiotic."

"Why?"

"*Why?* Because she's a good worker. I need her."

"You know what, Matt? You're thirty-one. At this point in your life I would much rather hear you say you need a woman sexually than as a good secretary."

Matt squeezed his eyes shut. "Here we go again!"

"I'm not getting any younger. Neither are you. I would like to have grandkids while I still have energy enough to bounce them on my knee."

"You might want grandkids now, but I can't afford

kids for another few years. Besides, you're the one who always told me not to get involved with a woman until I'm ready. So butt out.''

Wayne's face reddened, and he looked down at his green beans.

Matt was instantly repentant.

''Dad, I'm sorry, I…''

''No, it's all right. You're right. A man needs to be ready to get married and even more ready to have kids. If you think you're not there financially, then I support you.''

Matt said, ''Thanks.'' But he felt awful, really and truly awful. Not because he had insulted his dad, though he had. But more because he wasn't ready. And because he *wasn't* ready he couldn't give his dad the family he wanted.

Worse, he felt awful because he couldn't protect Sarah.

The next morning, Matt sat behind his desk feeling like the starship *Enterprise* on red alert. Grant had to pass through Sarah and Sunny's workstation to get to his office and if he said one word that Matt didn't like, Matt was pouncing. He couldn't save Sarah by dating her because he was her boss, but that didn't mean he would let her get involved with a man who had no in-tention of settling down. So far neither Grant nor Sarah had arrived, but Matt was ready.

Even as he finished that thought, Sarah turned the corner from the main entryway. As she had the day before, she walked down the hall to her office as if in slow motion. The thick curls of her beautiful red hair bounced around her. Her long legs ate up the space to her office as if it were nothing. Her navy-blue suit fit her as if it had been made for her. Her flawless makeup made her look like a model rather than an accounting assistant.

"Good morning, Matt!"

He cleared his throat. Without getting up from his seat he called, "Good morning."

Grant Lawson picked that precise second to walk down the corridor. Reading a newspaper and carrying a briefcase, he nearly walked into Sarah.

"Oh, I'm sorry!" he said, dropping his briefcase and grabbing her shoulders to right her when she swayed on her tall navy-blue shoes.

Sarah smiled at him. "It's okay. No harm done. I should know better than to stop in the hall."

Gazing into Sarah's eyes, Grant grinned and Matt's pulse began to hammer. He rose from his seat and rounded his desk. He was halfway to Sarah's workstation before he realized he had no clue what he would say, and no right to say anything anyway.

Grant stepped back. "I still should have been looking," he said, then picked up his briefcase. "Would you tell Sunny to buzz me the second she gets in? I'm closing my door today. I don't want to be disturbed."

Sarah turned and walked to her desk. "Sure. I'll be glad to."

Grant stuck his nose in his newspaper again. "Great. Thanks."

Matt stared at the scene, deciding he must have imagined anything flirtatious he'd thought he'd seen in the beginning of that mess. Not only did Sarah not look interested in Grant, but Grant didn't look interested in Sarah. A swell of relief filled Matt's chest, until he realized he really was jealous. And not just the I-wish-I-was-like-him kind of jealous. He was full-blown, man-woman jealous. And there wasn't a darned thing he could do about it.

"Do you need something, Matt?" Sarah asked curiously and Matt recognized that he had been standing in his doorway, staring at her, for at least thirty seconds.

He looked at her beautiful red hair cascading around her and at her pretty green eyes. In that second, he knew that if the situation were right, he would be dating her. And it didn't seem fair that he couldn't.

But, fair or not, it was life. Not dating a subordinate was a rule made not to protect bosses, but to protect the people who worked for them. Because he would never, ever, do anything to hurt Sarah, Matt turned and walked into his office without a word. He would get beyond this. He had to.

But as the morning wore on and the parade of men continued, Matt began to get tense. He also noticed something else. Not one other executive in this company seemed concerned about dating a subordinate. True, none of them was Sarah's immediate supervisor as Matt was. But they were still supervisors. And supervisors didn't date subordinates! They all should be staying the hell away from her.

The flirting and silliness went on throughout the afternoon, and Matt's irritation grew. The whole world seemed intent on thumbing its nose at rules Matt held sacred. He became more and more angry at the injustice of it, until he snapped at Carmella that night when she stopped in his office to deliver a copy of a confidential memo from the head of the company, Lloyd Winters.

"Sorry," he said, then ran his fingers through his short hair, spiking it.

Carmella smiled at him. "That's okay. It's nearly eight o'clock," she said, obviously referring to the fact that he was working late. Not only was the quarterly report due in six weeks, but also he did his staff review for Lloyd the first two weeks in September. "It's been a long day for you."

"Yeah. A long day made longer by the parade of men stopping by to flirt with my assistant."

Carmella grimaced. "I'll talk to her."

"It's not Sarah that's the problem. It's the guys coming to ogle her."

Carmella studied Matt for a second and he felt his face redden as she smiled knowingly. "You're not angry. You're jealous."

"I didn't say that."

"You didn't have to." She took a seat on one of the captain's chairs in front of Matt's desk and grinned at him as if this were some sort of game. "So, what are you going to do?"

"Nothing," he said, tossing his pencil to his desk, confused that he seemed to be the only reasonable person in this company since Sarah got her makeover. "In the first place, she's my assistant. Asking her out is a sexual harassment suit wait to happen."

"I don't think Sarah would…"

"It doesn't matter," Matt said, interrupting her, deciding that the entire office had gone around the bend and there was no sense trying to persuade Carmella with an argument she wouldn't understand. Particularly since he had a better argument up his sleeve. One she couldn't dispute. "There are more considerations here than just the boss/assistant thing. For one, I'm not in a position yet where I could ask somebody to marry me."

Carmella only stared at him. "Are you kidding?"

He stared back. "About what?"

"Oh, come on, Matt. I know you're one of those

people who likes to be prepared, but don't you think it's a bit overboard not dating a woman because you can't ask her to marry you?"

"No. Think this through, Carmella. Sarah's my assistant. If we date and break up, it will be a disaster. So, unless I'm planning to marry her, I can't date her."

"Ask her to move to another department."

"Still doesn't work. Even if I got her transferred, I couldn't consider asking someone to share my life with me when I'm not financially stable."

"With your job and your salary, you're certainly stable."

"Not stable enough."

Carmella chuckled. "What do you want? To be a millionaire?"

"Yes, before I'm forty. That's the plan."

Carmella gaped at him as if he were crazy. "And you won't stray from it even at the risk of losing a woman you like?"

"I would rather lose her up front, than have her divorce me because we have money troubles later."

Carmella stayed quiet for several seconds. Finally, she said, "You're too adamant. Too sure. There has to be a reason you've thought all this through."

Matt sighed. "There is."

"Want to tell me?"

"There's not much to tell. My parents split when I was ten because they were in debt up over their ears. My dad didn't have his degree when they got married, so he worked in a factory during the day and took classes at night. Money was always tight and all they did was fight. My first memories are of my parents fighting. My last memory of my mother is her slamming our kitchen door."

"You never saw her after she left?"

He shook his head. "I saw her, but I never talked to her. I never got the guts to ring her doorbell because I knew there was a good chance she wouldn't want to see me. She married a very wealthy man and didn't like to be reminded of being poor."

Carmella's eyes softened. "Her loss."

Matt shook his head. "*Our* loss. My dad missed her as much as I did. And he warned me a hundred times growing up that a man had to be prepared for marriage."

"I see."

"Well, even if you didn't get that part of it, there's another thing you're forgetting about this situation with Sarah. She's been "herself" for only a couple of days. Not long enough to really enjoy it. And that makes three good reasons for me to back off. First, she's my assistant. Second, I'm nowhere near financially ready for dating someone I can't risk breaking up with. And third, she's brand-new to being beautiful. There's a whole world out there for her to discover."

For several seconds Carmella remained silent, then she sighed. "You really have all the answers, don't you?"

"I have to."

"Okay," she said, rising from the seat in front of Matt's desk. "Suit yourself. But if I were you, I wouldn't be sitting on my laurels when another man is in hot pursuit of a woman I care about."

This time Matt laughed. "Actually, Carmella, one dozen roses don't mean a man's in hot pursuit."

Already on her way out the door, Carmella stopped and faced him. "You don't think so?"

"No. If somebody were really in hot pursuit of Sarah,

he would show himself. Make a move. At the very least send more flowers. She knocked herself out to look good for him and he's ignoring that.'' He caught Carmella's gaze. ''I think that speaks volumes.''

Chapter Three

The first thing Matt noticed when Sarah arrived the next morning was that her ivory-colored dress brought out the green in her eyes. The closer she got as she walked down the aisle toward her desk, the more he could see the vivid hue. But the closer she got the more he also sensed something wasn't quite right.

It wasn't until Sarah reached her desk that Matt realized her eyes might be rich, enticing green, almost jade, but they weren't bright with happiness as they had been on Tuesday morning. In spite of all the attention she was getting, she wasn't happy. Not the way she had been when she'd first arrived with her brand-new look. Then her eyes had virtually glowed. Not the way she had been before word spread that she had gotten a makeover and the vultures began to pounce.

Matt took another peek at the soft knit material of the clinging dress that rode nicely along her curves and showcased her great legs, and wished he could be the man she dressed up for. He would put the sparkle back in her eyes.

But he knew he couldn't. There was no guarantee a relationship between them would work, and the stakes were too high if they failed. He couldn't risk it. So he steadied himself for another day of unscheduled visits and general flirting from men, and, as he did, he suddenly understood Sarah's problem. If he was having trouble adjusting to the non-stop attention she was getting, Sarah probably felt as if she were drowning. Her inability to handle all the comments, compliments and ogling might actually be what had cost her the sparkle in her eyes.

Once again, however, he couldn't do anything about it. If she was unhappy being the new Sarah Morris, then everything he had told Carmella the night before held true but with a twist. Sarah might not need a chance to "enjoy" being the new her, but she did have to decide for herself if her new look was worth all the trouble it was causing. Even if Matt weren't her boss and had tons of money in the bank, he would have to let her alone.

He cast one more longing glance at her perfect legs, hoping she didn't let the vultures scare her off. He really believed what she had told him Tuesday morning—that this was the real Sarah—and he didn't want her to go back to being the timid woman in long dull suits just because too many men gave her too much attention. He hoped, really hoped, she would adjust to being this beautiful woman, rather than go back into her shell.

"Good morning, Matt."

He rose from his seat and walked to his door. "Good morning, Sarah." Normally, he would simply call out his greeting, but now that he recognized this wasn't easy for her, he didn't want to shout at her. Unfortunately, being so close to her caused all kinds of new feelings to rumble around inside him. Feelings that he couldn't explain. Feelings that he also couldn't seem to ignore. They held him captive, tongue-tied, unable to say anything to this woman he was supposed to know, but didn't. Not really.

Grant strode in, reading the *Boston Globe* as he walked. "Good morning," he said, raising his gaze from the newspaper to smile at Sarah. His blue eyes were bright and wolfish. His smile was definitely flirtatious. "Sure is one heck of a storm out there."

Sarah returned Grant's smile, but Matt's gut clenched as he spiraled further into the unfamiliar emotional territory that was becoming the norm in his life. Jealousy threaded through him, tightening his muscles and pumping adrenaline through his blood.

"Yes, it is one heck of a storm," Matt replied before Sarah could. He knew it was juvenile to answer when Grant was clearly talking to Sarah. But Matt couldn't stop himself. Which threw him into the even more unfamiliar territory of being out of control, unable to harness responses that he knew were just plain stupid. "I understand this is going to be one of our worst hurricane seasons, so we'll be getting lots of rain."

Oblivious to Matt's idiocy, Grant grunted in agreement as he walked into his office.

Sarah faced Matt again. Her beautiful green eyes had narrowed and Matt felt like a fool. A Neanderthal. Protecting someone he had no right to protect.

He sighed. "We have a lot to do today."

"I know," Sarah said, then turned away to flick on her computer monitor, as she did first thing every morning.

When she faced him again and smiled at him the way she usually did, Matt concluded she had dismissed what she'd seen happen between him and Grant. But he also realized something else. When she stepped into her normal routine, and behaved like the Sarah he knew, all of his feelings of jealousy and being out of control disappeared and he could behave normally, too.

He cleared his throat. "I like that dress," he said, because he did like her dress and he didn't want her switching back to her old wardrobe just because all the men at Wintersoft—including him, it seemed—had gone off the deep end.

She glanced down at the ivory knit creation. "Really? This is one of my old things. I bought it for a party thrown by one of my dad's friends."

"Which just goes to show you didn't change completely."

Her gaze sharpened. "Excuse me?"

"Well, with the new clothes and the new hair and…you know," he said, motioning with his hands, "makeup and stuff, you just seem like a whole different person. But wearing a dress from before proves you're not."

She laughed lightly, sounding like the Sarah Matt knew. The Sarah whose emphasis wasn't on the way she looked, but who she was. "I see what you're saying."

"I'm saying you're still yourself."

"Yes, I am."

Her reply and tone were so accommodating that Matt decided it was okay to give his entire opinion. "That's good because even though you might be worried that your new clothes are making a mess of your life, they aren't. It's other people's reactions and you shouldn't let that affect your decisions about how you dress. You look great, Sarah. And you're still yourself. It's other people who have the problem.''

She considered that a second, then said, ''I know. I like my new clothes, and I have more confidence, so I'm going to stick it out. Pretty soon the fury will die down.''

Matt nearly breathed a sigh of relief. ''Let's hope,'' he said, satisfied that he had found a way to keep her from making a mistake by going back to her old jackets, big skirts and braided hair.

''Yeah, let's hope,'' Sarah echoed, watching Matt as he went into his office. The way he had stayed away from her for the past two days, making room for the parade of men who had walked by her desk, flirted with her and even asked her out, almost proved he'd sent her those roses to nudge her into getting a makeover so that other men would notice her.

But this morning she could tell he wasn't entirely happy with his plan. She would have to be blind not to notice the little spurt of jealousy when Grant arrived. And she'd have to be stupid not to realize Matt had put his stamp of approval on her makeover with the things he'd said once Grant had slipped into his office.

She didn't precisely think Matt had suddenly acquired romantic feelings for her. But she did believe he regretted his plan to send her flowers and wanted their relationship to go back to where it had been Friday afternoon before the flowers had arrived. He didn't want her to revert to wearing her old clothes, but he did want their relationship to shift back to normal.

As the morning progressed, he behaved so much like the boss he had been for the past year that when he left for his meeting with Lloyd Winters an hour later, Sarah decided that her conclusion was correct. They were back to being the comfortable boss and assistant they had been before she got the roses. They were friends again, which wasn't really what she wanted, but it was better than being embarrassed that he sent her flowers to get a makeover for another man!

Sarah genuinely believed everything had been straightened out between them, until ten o'clock when the second dozen roses arrived. These were red.

"Oh, my gosh, Penny! Look at them."

Penny sighed with awe. "They're beautiful," she whispered as if the twelve bloodred blooms lying in the florist's box were something sacred.

Sarah could only stare at them. They *were* beautiful. They were the most beautiful flowers she had ever seen and for a good two minutes they completely confused her. She couldn't figure out why Matt sent her flowers again. Particularly since the first dozen had only made a mess of their lives.

She glanced up at Penny. "Has Carmella seen these?"

"No, she's in Mr. Winter's office straightening up, while he's at the appointment with Matt."

Sarah rose from her seat. "I've got to show her." She took two steps toward the corridor that led to Lloyd Winters' office, but stopped as a swell of coworkers approached her.

"We heard you got flowers again!" Ariana Fitzpatrick, public relations manager said. Pregnant with twins, Ariana's five-foot-four-inch frame looked overburdened, but the strain didn't dampen the brightness in her hazel eyes. "Are they from your secret admirer?"

In all the confusion, Sarah had forgotten to look at the card. She set the flowers on her desk and fumbled with the envelope. The card read, Love, Your Secret Admirer.

Love?

Everybody gasped with appreciation, but Sarah's heart rate sped up and she felt flushed. Love? It didn't make any sense for Matt to send her flowers with a card that said love. But she remembered the way he'd stuttered over her new look Tuesday morning, remembered his jealousy over Grant, remembered that he had told her he was glad she had changed her look but hadn't changed her personality, and she wondered. Maybe she'd misinterpreted their entire conversation that morning?

If she looked at that discussion from the opposite perspective, everything changed. If she recognized his jealousy as attraction then she would have to consider that her makeover might have forced him to see her as a woman rather than just an assistant. Plus, he might have reminded her that she was the same person to validate that his feelings for her were more than physical.

She blinked, overwhelmed by her realizations. If these flowers and this card were different from the first ones he'd sent, it was because the message was different. He didn't want her to keep her makeover so she'd be attractive to other men. He wanted her for himself.

Awareness shivered through her, causing her to draw another conclusion. If he said he loved her, he meant it and he would want everything that entailed. They could be *making love* before this day was done!

The thought of touching her lips to his, caressing his broad shoulders, being caressed by him, shot a tingle of excitement through her. She'd thought about kissing him before—she'd dreamed about it—but never with this overwhelming sense that it was really about to happen.

A hush fell over the crowd and Sarah glanced up from the card in time to see the people part and form a path up the hall. At its end was Matt.

"What's this?" he asked, walking toward Sarah's desk.

She peeked up at him. Their gazes caught and she knew her moment of truth had arrived. If he'd sent them, she would know. Even if he couldn't admit it in front of this crowd, she would see it in the expression in his eyes or hear it in something he said. She nodded toward the box on her desk.

Matt glanced at the roses. "Oh." He caught her gaze again, then nervously asked, "No note this time?"

Her eyes locked with his; she said, "Yeah, there's a note."

"And..." he said, encouraging her to reply.

And? she thought, staring at him. Was he asking for an answer? Did he want her to say, "I love you, too?" For Pete's sake! Not only was that rushing things a bit, but they were in a crowd!

Luckily, Ariana answered for her. "It says, 'Love, Your Secret Admirer'!" she said, and sighed with feminine appreciation.

Giggles erupted, along with a cacophony of speculation on what that particular signature meant, who the secret admirer could be, and why he was sending flowers instead of asking Sarah out.

Matt's gaze skittered back to Sarah's. Then he glanced at the flowers, looked at the card she held in her trembling hand, peered at the noisy crowd of onlookers and walked away, into his office, and closed the door.

Sarah dropped her head to her hand. Damn it!

"Could everybody please go back to your desk?" she called because she needed to think this through.

"Yes, how about everybody going back to his or her desk?"

That question was spoken by Lloyd Winters, and for the second time a hush fell over the group of onlookers.

Tall, white-haired Lloyd said only one more word, "Now," and everybody scattered. Then he turned his big blue eyes on Sarah. "What's this?"

She cleared her throat. "Someone's sending me flowers."

Lloyd picked up one of the bright red blooms. "Beautiful roses."

"Yes. They are."

"Red's the color you send for love." He smiled. "My late wife told me that." He sighed and set the bloom back into the box. "Well, enjoy this," he said, smiling benignly at her. "You deserve it. But no more small gatherings every time you get a delivery. Who knows how long this could go on."

Sarah laughed. "Okay."

When Lloyd was gone, Sarah glanced at Matt's closed door in dismay. He didn't need to have seen Lloyd to find out what had happened beside her desk after he left. There were only a hundred and fifty Wintersoft employees, and Lloyd Winters treated everyone like family. By noon, it would be the talk of the building that Lloyd had stopped by to see her flowers. By twelve-fifteen, the discussion would move on to how he hadn't exactly reprimanded her, but had cautioned her about drawing a crowd with her deliveries. By twelve-thirty there would be a betting pool on whether or not the poor sap who had sent her the flowers would strike again.

Which meant there would be no more flowers. Matt wouldn't do anything that went against his boss's wishes.

But it also meant that even if Matt was embarrassed, concerned about gossip, or afraid of jeopardizing their work relationship, she was going to have to get him to own up to these.

Behind the closed door of his office Matt fumed. The first dozen roses were easy enough to rationalize. Somebody liked Sarah. That was good. After an entire year in Boston with hardly any recognition at all, having someone send her flowers was a big boost to her morale. He had approved of that. Particularly since several days had gone by without the guy identifying himself. Which meant the flowers were just a sweet gesture, somebody being kind to a woman who needed a boost.

But now the idiot had struck again. This time with red roses that all but screamed approval of her new sexy look. He wouldn't be surprised if the lovesick fool called her tonight, made a date, took her to dinner and…

He couldn't finish his thought. It made him want to choke someone.

''Matt?''

Matt spun away from the wall of windows behind his desk to face Emily Winters who had opened his door and popped her head inside. Though her big blue eyes were just like her dad's, the similarity of appearance stopped there. Her long dark hair was the complete antithesis of Lloyd's short white locks. Professionally, however, she was every bit as sharp as her father was.

"My dad said you were supposed to join us in his office so you guys can brief me on this morning's meeting." She stepped inside and closed the door. "Should I tell him you're unexpectedly busy?"

Matt sighed with disgust. He had forgotten all about this just because Sarah got flowers. He was pathetic. "No. I'm on my way."

She smiled. "Okay," but she paused and added, "Is something wrong?"

"No. No. Everything's fine."

She peered at him. "You sure? Your face is all red and you look...well, flustered."

"I'm fine," he said and wanted to kick himself. This was exactly the kind of situation he had spent his life avoiding. Men who went all weird and crazy over women ended up screwing up at work, losing their jobs and all kinds of other flaky things. He would not be one of those men. Especially not around the woman who would be taking over when her dad retired. He had to pull himself together and behave like the professional he knew he was.

"I'm fine. Let's go. Your dad and I have lots to tell you."

"So I heard," Emily said as she led Matt into Sarah's office. "Great roses, Sarah," she complimented as they walked past Sarah's desk. Sarah had arranged the flowers in a vase, and the sweet scent filled the air.

Sarah's gaze meandered over to Matt's. "Thanks, these are even more beautiful than the white ones. They're perfect," she added, holding his gaze. "I *love* them."

Knowing this was his big opportunity to make himself look like a normal man who didn't mind that his assistant was getting flowers from a secret admirer and who most certainly wouldn't let *her* getting roses mess up *his* work performance, Matt straightened and smiled broadly at his assistant. "That's great! Exactly what a woman should say when she gets flowers like that." He turned and began walking again. "I'll be in Mr. Winters's office for the next hour or so."

Sarah all but danced with joy after he left. She had done it. She'd told him how she felt and he'd smiled. He liked her. Actually, he said he loved her. Well, his *card* said he loved her. And that was pushing things.

So the first chance she got she was going to slow him down. No matter how much she felt for him, she wasn't ready for what he seemed to want, so when they were alone—and she suspected they would be soon—she would tell him that now that their cards were out on the table they needed to slow things down a bit.

But though Sarah wanted to go slowly, she had no idea that Matt would drop their speed to a crawl. Or, worse yet, bring them to a screeching halt. He didn't speak a personal word to her when he returned from his meeting with Emily and Lloyd Winters and wasn't around when Sarah left for the day. Though she'd waited an entire fifteen minutes past quitting time to give him a chance to ask if he could come over to her apartment, he never returned from wherever he went about three o'clock that afternoon. He also didn't call her that night.

Friday when Sarah arrived at work, Matt's door was closed. She concluded that that meant he was writing the performance reviews he would be providing Lloyd. She knew a smart assistant would realize Matt needed quiet and privacy to get everything done. She even took her roses home at lunchtime to stem the tide of visitors and well-wishers.

But that afternoon, Sarah knew the games would stop. Grant had left Thursday afternoon for two weeks of out-of-the-office meetings. Sunny was leaving at noon. Sarah and Matt would be totally alone in their section of the office floor, and Matt had the perfect opportunity to ask her out or say whatever it was he wanted to say but couldn't because they were always surrounded by people.

In the lounge, Sarah adjusted her silky emerald-green skirt and a simple white blouse, which she accented with a fat jade pendant that fell to just above her breasts. She looked professional, but pretty, and realized that her outfit more or less said that they were settling in. She wouldn't be going overboard with clothes anymore and he wouldn't have to send her any more flowers.

All he had to do was own up to the ones he'd already sent.

But when she returned to her office, his door was closed again. She knew he probably had plenty of work to do and turned on her computer monitor, sat at her desk and began to input the new figures for the revised quarterly statement.

At two o'clock, she realized Matt had probably forgotten that Sunny was out of the office that afternoon and she knocked on his door, then pushed it open.

"Hey," she said, about to tell him that there was no need to have his door closed, but she stopped abruptly when she saw that his shirt looked as if he had slept in it and his hair was sticking out in all directions. "Did you sleep here last night?" she teased.

He waved her off. "No. I'm just having a rough day.

Would you mind?'' he asked, indicating that he wanted her to leave. "And close the door behind you.''

"That's actually why I popped in. Sunny's off for the afternoon. You can leave your door open.''

He shook his head. "Close it.''

"I took the roses home,'' she said, figuring that he was still bothered by the throngs of admirers who stopped at her desk.

His scowl deepened.

"I mean it. It's quiet as a meadow out here. There's no need to close your door.''

"Close it,'' he said firmly and Sarah did.

But the longer she sat at her desk, the angrier she got. It was almost as if he was blaming her for the noise and confusion generated by flowers *he* had sent. At five o'clock she was officially angry. So much so that she decided to wait for the rest of the staff to leave and confront him. Because it was Friday, the Wintersoft floor was quiet a little after six and she pushed her way into his office again.

"Sarah, I said I wanted the door closed...''

"I know and it infuriates me. You would think it was my fault that I got flowers and everybody and her dog decided it was okay to stand at my desk and chat for a few minutes.''

"I know it's not your fault.''

"You're damned right it's not!''

For thirty seconds, Matt only stared at her. Part of him was writhing in delight. If she wanted a fight about those flowers, he was just the guy to give it to her. Part of him was still trying to look like a normal person who hadn't spent the past few days alternating between being furious that somebody was trying to steal Sarah right out from under his nose and being aghast that it seemed that everybody in this company condoned Sarah going out with a virtual stranger. Everybody they knew had stopped and commented on her flowers. Most had speculated about who could have sent them. Every man in the company had signed up for the pool in the break room, speculating on when the guy would reveal himself.

He just wanted to spit.

But he wouldn't.

"Go home, Sarah."

"No. I think it's time we had this out."

"Had what out?"

"Ever since the second flowers arrived you've been treating me like I have the plague!"

"I've been busy."

"You've never locked yourself behind closed doors when you were busy before."

"This time is different."

"The only thing that's different is the flowers."

He sighed. "We're back to that."

"Yes. I want to talk about them."

"I don't." He couldn't. How could he tell her he was jealous when he hadn't had a romantic thought toward her until the first ones were delivered? Worse, how could he tell her he was jealous when he had no right to be and no intention of doing anything about it since good bosses didn't romance their subordinates?

Completely catching him off guard, Sarah marched around his desk, swung his chair around and trapped him in his seat by anchoring her hands on both arms of his chair. "I do."

In their entire work association, Matt didn't think they had ever been this close. He could smell the light floral scent of her cologne, see the flecks of gold in her green eyes, see the plump smoothness of her lips and feel the heat of her anger as it emanated from her.

Technically, she had no right to be angry with him. She should be thanking him for being a gentleman.

"You should be thanking me."

She stared at him. "For what?"

"For being a gentleman."

"What the heck is that supposed to mean?"

"It means that if we were in any other kind of circumstance I would be doing this right now." Before she had a chance to react, Matt caught her hands, lifted them from his chair and swiveled her so she fell into his lap. Then he lowered his head and kissed her.

Chapter Four

Sarah thought she would die from the sheer pleasure of kissing Matt. His lips were warm and tasted sweet, but it wasn't the physical sensation of kissing him that totally disarmed her. It was the bits and pieces of his personality that shone through in a few seconds of touching. He wanted her, there was no doubt about that. His rough demanding kiss proved it.

But as quickly as he'd flipped her onto his lap, he flipped her off, righted her and turned her toward his door.

"You have to go. I have to go," he said, grabbing his briefcase as he pulled her out of his office and into hers. He caught her jacket and shoulder-strap purse from the back of her desk chair and all but dragged her to the elevator.

Twice she tried to say something as the elevator descended, but the words got stuck in her throat. Matt pulled her out of the building, then deposited her at her bus stop just as her bus arrived. He said a quick goodbye and disappeared into the Friday night crowd that hustled its way home.

Sarah stood on the curb in open-mouthed confusion. The bus door opened. She got on, took a seat and then stared into space.

He'd kissed her. And it was fabulous and he couldn't take it back or pretend he didn't know what she was talking about the way he did about the flowers.

Saturday morning Matt walked up to the door of Sarah's apartment and, without a second's hesitation, pushed the bell. He'd debated this situation the entire night before, pacing, shaking his head at his stupidity and cursing himself for being weak-willed. After hours of tossing and turning, he knew what he had to do. Apologize. Assure her it wouldn't happen again. And hope she didn't file sexual harassment charges.

Sarah answered her door wearing a pink chenille robe that highlighted the red hue of her sleep-tousled hair. Matt's gaze fell from her wicked-looking locks, down the V of flesh left exposed by the closure of the robe, to the nice curve of her waist at the cinch of the belt and to the long length of leg exposed because the robe was a shortie, not floor-length.

Every thought he had fell out of his head.

Sarah grabbed his arm and tugged him inside. "Come in! Come in!"

When she let go, Matt stayed exactly where he stood, dumbfounded that he had put them in another compromising position.

"Coffee?"

He took two paces back, getting close to the door again. The last thing he needed to do was spend time in her company now that he knew how soft her lips were, how good it felt to kiss her. Particularly since only one thin robe separated him from smooth, sleep-warmed skin.

"No." He took another step back. "Sarah, this isn't going to take long. I'm just here to apologize."

"Apologize?"

"I shouldn't have kissed you. I was out of line." He shrugged, trying to look unaffected, as if just thinking about that kiss didn't make him long to do it again. "I don't even have a logical excuse."

Sarah's brow furrowed. "Excuse?"

"For kissing you."

"Normally, a man kisses a woman because he likes her."

Since pretending he was unaffected wasn't working, Matt decided honesty had to be the better route. After all, she was his assistant. If he told her his problem, he should be able to enlist her help to keep himself in line.

"That's true. All of it. Every part of it. I did kiss you and I do like you. But I'm your boss and I'm not supposed to kiss you."

This time Sarah frowned. "Why not?"

"Because we work together and people who work together and have romantic relationships find themselves in hot water. You weren't around five years ago, but Emily Winters dated a former Wintersoft executive named Todd Baxter. She even married him. That ended in disaster. Todd decided to quit." He shook his head. "I don't want to end up like that."

Sarah took a step closer and smiled at him. "You're saying you think a relationship between us would fail?"

Staring into her pretty jade-green eyes, Matt almost didn't care, but he knew it was wrong to feel that way.

"I can't predict the future, and I'm not willing to take the risk with your career or mine."

Sarah fiddled with his shirt collar and little goose bumps of energy danced across his neck. "Actually, Matt, after that kiss I don't think there's much chance that we'd fail."

Matt sucked in his breath and took another step backward. "There's still no guarantee that we wouldn't, and I'm not willing to take the risk. We work together. I like you as my assistant. I *need* you as my assistant. I won't risk losing you."

He watched the expression in her eyes change as his reasoning began to sink in. When her hands fell to her sides, he knew she understood that he meant what he said and wouldn't change his mind.

"Then what was that kiss about? Better yet, why the heck send me flowers if you have no intention of following through?"

Matt looked at her. "I didn't send those flowers."

"Of course you did! Who else would? Who else even knows me in this town?"

Suddenly everything that hadn't made sense to Matt for the past week, all the odd comments, the strange reactions, even Sarah provoking him to kiss her the night before fell into place.

He gentled his voice. "I don't know, Sarah. But it wasn't me."

The color drained from Sarah's face and panic filled Matt. The last thing he wanted to do was hurt her, but if things between them had heated up because she thought he was her secret admirer, then he had to be honest to stop all this craziness.

She took a step back and pressed her hand to her chest. "Oh, God! I'm so embarrassed!"

"It's not a big deal," Matt said, but from the look on her face, he knew it was. Not only had he not sent the flowers, but he had never for one second considered that she might think it was him, and she probably felt foolish for having imagined things that weren't there.

"I'm sure the guy who sent them is very nice," he soothed, deciding that shifting her focus away from him—away from *them*—and onto the positive aspects of the flowers was the only way to stop her misery. "He's probably better for you than I am anyway."

"Right," Sarah said, trying to sound unaffected, but she was dying. Remembering how she'd stormed his office the night before, determined to get him to admit he'd sent her the flowers, she just wished she could disappear.

"That's all part of why I'm sorry that I kissed you," Matt continued, clearly trying to make her feel better, but only making her feel worse. She'd virtually thrown herself at him the night before. "This guy who is sending you flowers obviously likes you and is probably ready to make a move. He's getting you ready for that. My kissing you just confuses things."

Again, his explanation proved he'd never had a romantic thought toward her and, like a starry-eyed schoolgirl, she'd pushed him to do things he never would have thought of on his own. She wanted to crawl into a hole and die.

Since she couldn't do that, she settled for getting him out of her home. "Right. That makes perfect sense. Good sense." She walked to her apartment door and opened it. "I'll see you Monday then."

Relief lit Matt's handsome face. "Really?"

"Of course! I'm fine! It was just a little misunderstanding."

Matt's smile of relief grew. "Good. I'll see you Monday."

The minute the door closed behind Matt, Sarah dropped her head to her hands. She had just made a colossal fool of herself and she wasn't really sure she could go to work on Monday morning, because she didn't believe she could ever face Matt again.

The knowledge that she'd made a fool of herself worked on Sarah so much that by Monday morning, she knew what she had to do. She dressed in one of her old blue suits, braided what was left of her hair and even dug out her old glasses. Her thick, comfortable shoes squeaked as she walked through the Wintersoft lobby.

When she arrived at the reception desk, Penny stared at her in dismay. "Sarah? What happened?"

Sarah smiled as brightly as she could. "Nothing. Why do you think something happened?"

She walked through the reception area, through the oak double doors behind it and into the huge space that housed Carmella's workstation, fronting the corresponding double doors for Lloyd Winters's office.

Carmella looked up from her desk and dropped her pencil. "Oh, Sarah! What the heck happened?"

Sarah smiled at her and pushed her big glasses up her nose. "Nothing."

"Something happened!" Carmella said, picking up her phone receiver and pressing a button. "Get up here!" she said, before disconnecting the call and rushing over to Sarah. "Lloyd has an out-of-office meeting this morning."

"I know. He's with Matt."

"So, we're going to use his office for a little chat. Emily's on her way down."

"I don't need to chat," Sarah said as Carmella led her into Lloyd's office.

The room was huge but every inch was put to good use. A round conference table and four chairs sat to the right of the door. To the left were bookcases. A bar sat beside the leather sofa-and-chair arrangement across from Lloyd's big desk. Behind the bar was a mahogany spiral staircase leading down to Emily's office.

Carmella settled Sarah on the burgundy sofa and poured her a cup of coffee. By the time Sarah had a mug in her hands, Emily was climbing up the staircase behind the bar.

When she saw Sarah, her mouth fell open in dismay. "Oh, no! What happened?"

Sarah laughed lightly. "Nothing happened!"

Emily sat beside her on the sofa. "Sarah, you are either absolutely crazy or in deep denial. What happened?"

Sarah drew a long breath. "Matt's not the secret admirer."

Carmella sat on the other side of Sarah. "He told you that?"

Sarah nodded.

Emily slid her arm around Sarah's shoulders. "Did he just say it or did something lead up to that?"

"He kissed me and came to my apartment to apologize. I couldn't understand why he'd be apologizing for wanting a relationship with me when he's been leading up to kissing me with the flowers he had been sending, and he told me he wasn't the one sending the flowers."

Emily frowned. "Oh."

But Carmella laughed. "So what? He might not have sent the flowers, but you're missing the big picture here. *He kissed you!*"

"Yes, he did!" Emily agreed. "And do you know what that means?"

Sarah shook her head.

"You must really be getting under his skin for him to have lost control like that!" Emily said with an airy laugh. "Oh, this is great!"

"I don't think so," Sarah said in dismay.

"Sure it is," Carmella insisted. "By getting him to kiss you, technically, you did what you set out to do when you originally got this makeover. Because you thought it was Matt who sent you the flowers, it was Matt's attention you were trying to get and you got it."

Sarah glanced from Carmella to Emily. "So I didn't make a fool of myself?"

"Heck no!" Emily said. "What you did was succeed in spades!"

"Right," Carmella agreed. "And now that you have Matt's attention, you can't lose it by going back to square one," she added, pointing to Sarah's old suit.

"Okay," Sarah agreed. This time her laugh was genuine. "I get it. I panicked."

"Happens to the best of us," Emily assured her as she rose. "The trick to this is to act totally unfazed. Sure, Matt might not have sent you the flowers, but you now know he's interested."

"But he doesn't want to be."

"Doesn't matter," Carmella assured Sarah. "You go home and change. Come back looking sexy and confident and Matt will eventually work through his reasons for being against a relationship. Just be patient and calm and he'll come around."

"Really?"

"Absolutely," Emily and Carmella said simultaneously.

* * *

Walking to the bus stop, Sarah saw the wisdom of Emily and Carmella's reasoning. By the time she stepped into her apartment, she was relaxed and enthusiastic again. She applied her makeup, put in her contacts and curled her hair, feeling wonderful about herself. But after she slid into a moss-green suit with a white silk blouse, she stopped and stared at her reflection.

She really was this woman now. She really felt more comfortable dressed in pretty clothes. She really did like herself. She liked the way she looked. She liked having confidence. She knew she was intelligent and, in her own way, wise.

So what the heck was she doing chasing after a man who didn't want her? Particularly since there was somebody who did want her.

When she thought of the secret admirer who had sent her flowers, Sarah felt a twinge of guilt. Some sweet man had seen the real her and nudged her to let go a little bit and become the person she was intended to be. But instead of trying to find *him* or exercising patience until *he* announced himself, Sarah was still longing for Matt.

She'd even given Matt credit for something this sweet, sincere flower sender had done. In a way, she was rejecting him the same way Matt had rejected her after their Friday-night kiss.

And that just wasn't right.

When she arrived at work dressed in her slim green suit, wearing makeup, feeling like the confident woman she knew she was supposed to be, Sarah walked directly into Matt's office.

"No hard feelings."

He peeked up. "No?"

She smiled and shook her head. "I had a revelation this morning."

He leaned back in his seat. "Oh, yeah?"

"Yeah. I felt bad that you regretted kissing me. In fact, I felt so bad I was going to revert to my old suits and glasses."

Matt winced. "Sarah…"

She waved her hand in dismissal. "Oh, don't worry! That's all part of my revelation. This morning I saw that the same way I've had a crush on you for months…"

"You've had a crush on me?"

"It doesn't make any difference," she said, brushing off his question. "Because when I was thinking about the crush I had on you, I realized this morning that if I ignored my secret admirer, I would make him feel awful. The same way I felt awful over the weekend."

"I didn't mean to make you feel awful."

"I know. And I even think your rejecting me was the right thing to do, because now I can do a little investigating, and find this guy and give him a chance."

Matt leaned back in his chair. Saturday morning he had said good things about the secret admirer to make her feel better, but with her sudden intent to go looking for her mystery man, Matt remembered his other misgivings—that everybody in the office was thrilled by her getting flowers from a stranger.

"You're going looking for a guy who doesn't have the guts to face you, but sends you flowers anonymously?"

"I think it's romantic."

"I think it's dangerous."

Sarah frowned. "Matt, didn't you hear what I just said? I felt bad this weekend, and if I don't at least make an attempt to find the guy sending me roses I'm going to be making somebody else feel that way."

"So you're pinning this on me?"

"No, I'm just making a comparison. This has nothing to do with you."

But Matt couldn't help but feel that it did. In fact, as the day wore on and he realized both her high comfort level with him and her sincerity about finding her secret admirer were real, not a pretense, he had the feeling he had thrown her to the lions.

As she gathered her things to leave, he ambled to her desk. "Why don't we have dinner tonight?"

She smiled prettily, kindly. Not at all like a woman interested in him romantically. "I don't think that would be a good idea."

"Actually, Sarah, I want to talk a bit more about your decision to find your secret admirer."

She laughed. "I don't think there's anything else to talk about."

"Sure there is. For one, we really don't know who this man is."

She laughed again. "That's what makes it exciting."

The music of her laughter caused ripples of pleasure to skitter down Matt's spine. Right from the beginning, he had liked the new enthusiastic, confident Sarah. She was light, bubbly and so easy to be around he couldn't believe he had ever thought her backward. Still, her newfound self-assurance could also get her into trouble. And it was his fault because his reaction to kissing her had now pushed her in the direction of looking for her secret admirer.

"Don't forget exciting has two sides. There's good

exciting and bad exciting. You're assuming finding this guy will be a good thing. But what if he's a stalker?''

Sarah only stared at him. ''You know, you started this with your lecture about changing myself enough that a man who was interested in me would get the message that I wanted to be approached. Don't go spoiling it with your negative talk!''

''It's not negative talk. It's common sense. You could be feeling sorry for and planning to get involved with a stalker.''

Sarah planted her fists on her hips. ''And even if I were, you wouldn't have any right to stop me!''

With that she stormed out and Matt combed his fingers through his short hair, causing it to spike. Furious with himself because he knew he had approached that all wrong, he returned to his desk. He fell to his chair and sat back, sighing with frustration. He didn't have a clue what he should do, but he did have the sense that he had to do something because—like it or not—he had instigated her search for the secret admirer by kissing her.

There was a knock on his doorframe and Matt looked up to see Carmella standing at the entryway. ''Lloyd looked over this first draft of the second section of the quarterly report. His changes are marked,'' she said as she laid the draft on Matt's desk.

He blew his breath out on a long sigh. ''Thanks.''

Carmella smiled. ''Anything wrong?''

''No, everything's fine with the quarterly. It's actually ahead of schedule.''

''I wasn't talking about the quarterly. I was talking about you. Personally. Your hair looks like you combed it with a chain saw.''

Because Carmella was already in the loop on this,

Matt admitted, "Sarah is going to try to find her secret admirer."

Carmella frowned. "I didn't know that."

Hearing the confusion in her voice, Matt felt he had found an ally. "I think it's dangerous."

Carmella slid her hip on the corner of Matt's desk, clearly interested in the discussion. "I can't imagine why she's doing it."

Matt sighed. "It's my fault. I told her that I wasn't her secret admirer and that I wasn't interested in her."

Carmella appeared to consider that. "Well, if you're not interested, then I don't see what your problem is. I think she's within her rights to go looking for her secret admirer."

"But we don't know who this guy is! He sends flowers with cryptic cards that he doesn't sign. In some circles he would be considered a stalker. For all we know, he's some guy in prison who got her name and Wintersoft's address off the Internet!"

Carmella sighed. "All right. I see what you're saying." She paused and caught Matt's gaze. "But the truth is, you told me last Wednesday evening that you were interested in her. You could very well stop her search for this guy just by admitting it."

Matt stared at her. "Carmella, if you remember that discussion so well, you should also remember I told you that I'm not allowed to be interested in her. She's my subordinate. If things didn't work out, how the heck would we work together?"

"What if they did work out?"

"Then the rest of my staff could accuse me of favoritism."

Carmella laughed and rose from her perch on Matt's

desk. "That's right. You're the guy with all the answers."

"And no matter how I crunch the numbers they don't add up. I'm not allowed to date her, Carmella, and I'm staying away for her sake as well as mine."

"I see."

"Yeah. You sound convinced, too."

"Really. I understand what you're saying," Carmella assured him. "It is a bad situation." She smiled and turned to leave his office.

Matt sighed, unable to just let the topic go unresolved. "Especially since she's now going after a stalker."

Carmella stopped halfway to his door. "If you're that positive that she's about to get herself into trouble, there is one way for you to make sure she doesn't."

"What's that?"

"Help her."

"Help her?"

"Yes, the best way for you to control this situation and to make sure she doesn't get into any trouble is for you to join her in her search for her secret admirer. Then, if you find him and you decide he is a stalker, an ax murderer or even just a garden variety weirdo, you can lead her away from him."

"I get it."

Carmella smiled. "The trick to this, though, Matt, will be to be by her side every time she goes looking."

That gave Matt a twinge of warning. Lately, every minute he spent in Sarah's company he found another reason to like her. But surely, he could control his hormones for the few days or weeks it would take to find this guy and make sure Sarah was safe?

Piece of cake.

Chapter Five

Stifling a groan, Matt held the door for Sarah as she stepped into the florist's shop late Saturday afternoon. She had dressed in low-riding jeans and a short-sleeved white blouse to accommodate the change of weather from cold and rainy to bright and sunny, and probably didn't realize how feminine she looked in the simple outfit, or the way her jeans accented the sway of her hips when she walked. But Matt certainly noticed, and it was driving him crazy. He had had a twinge of warning when Carmella suggested he help Sarah, but he was now totally convinced this was a mistake. This was only the first day of their secret admirer search and already he was having trouble.

He watched the graceful swing of her hips as she walked up to the desk and pulled out the card from the first flower delivery, looking sweet and innocent yet still incredibly sexy, and, again, he almost groaned. This was truly a mistake.

"Hi, I'm Sarah Morris. I got flowers—white roses,"

she qualified, smiling at the memory, "from somebody last Friday. Then on Thursday, I got a dozen red roses. They were both from your shop. Is there any way I can get the name of the person who sent them?"

The petite clerk behind the desk sighed. College-age and reading a thick textbook, she obviously didn't appreciate being disturbed. "I'm not allowed to give out that information."

"Is your manager here?" Sarah asked, still smiling.

"Yeah, she's in the back. I'll get her." The clerk walked to the curtain-covered doorway behind her. "June!" she yelled, then returned and continued reading her book.

Sarah stepped away from the counter. "We'll just browse while we wait," she said to the clerk, who shrugged and said, "Whatever."

"Friendly staff," Matt muttered, ambling over to a table filled with floral arrangements. Silk replicas of the bouquets that could be made to order sat in a pyramidal grouping. "I can see why your stalker picked this place."

"He's not a stalker."

"You don't know that."

"And you don't know that he is," Sarah said and turned her attention to the flowers because, Matt was sure, she didn't want to hear this lecture again. But as he also inspected the various styles of bouquets and arrangements, another, better argument against Sarah's secret admirer struck him.

"He also isn't very imaginative."

Sarah faced him. Her green eyes were cool and wary, but at least Matt had her attention. "What kind of crack is that?"

"It's a perfectly legitimate observation. Look," he

said, pointing to an arrangement of roses, lilies and some kind of accent flower Matt couldn't name. "He could have sent you this. Instead he picked boring roses. The same old flower everybody sends."

"That arrangement *is* pretty," Sarah admitted grudgingly.

"It's more than pretty. It makes a statement."

Sarah only stared at him. "A statement?"

"Yes, if he had sent you these, with the different kinds of flowers, he would have been saying that he thinks you have a multi-layered personality."

That made Sarah laugh. "I get it. This is your idea of humor."

"I'm not being funny. I'm serious. When a guy sends flowers, especially if he's not signing his name, he should be giving clues about how he feels. Like these," Matt said, directing her to an arrangement of calla lilies. "These are flowers you see around sometimes, but they still look exotic." He paused, studied the flowers again, then added, "This is probably what I would have sent."

Sarah cast him a completely puzzled look. "Really?"

"Absolutely," Matt said, feeling he had finally found the avenue to make his point. "They're beautiful flowers, so I would be saying you're beautiful. But they're also exotic. Kind of unusual. Normal, but unusual."

"You think I'm unusual?"

"I think you're *exotic,*" he corrected, then slid his finger along the petal of the silk flower. "Exotic means you're real but with a twist. Something special makes you you."

Watching him caress the flower, Sarah fought a shiver. Not just because he thought her exotic, but also because his touch was gentle, almost reverent. As if he were touching her. The shiver passed through her again and she raised her eyes to meet Matt's.

"Thanks."

Matt smiled. "You're welcome."

Not wanting to make the mistake again of reading more into what he said than he intended, Sarah looked away and busied herself with another floral arrangement. "No one's ever called me exotic."

He laughed. "I'm surprised I said it myself, but once I had I knew I was right. Carmella and Emily might have put you into the same kind of clothes worn by every other woman in Boston, but you bring your own flavor to them, because at your core you're uniquely you. You're mature and feisty, both of which make you strong. But your strength also makes you sexy."

Again, Sarah stared at him in complete disbelief. She could believe that he saw her differently than anybody else did, but she was in disbelief that he had guts enough to say it. His words were romantic. Beautiful. Almost poetic. Especially for an accountant. It seemed as if he had looked beyond her surface appearance, and liked her soul and her sexuality more than her new outfits.

As she stood staring at Matt, a short, middle-aged woman approached them. Dressed in jeans and a grubby T-shirt that announced that Florists Do It In The Garden, she looked as though she had spent the morning filling orders.

"Hi, I'm June. I own the store. Janine tells me you were looking to get the name of somebody who sent you flowers."

Matt took the card from Sarah and handed it to June. "Yes, my assistant got flowers last Friday. This card with your store name was attached, and we were wondering if you could tell us who sent them.''

Though Sarah heard everything Matt said to the storeowner, her mind was still on the very poetic, very sweet way he had told her she was exotic, and she wondered if she shouldn't cancel her secret-admirer search. The way he saw her proved he had some kind of feelings for her. Probably more than even he himself realized. Maybe if she just had a little patience with him, he'd fall in love with her.

But June said something that caused Matt to say, "Great!" and before Sarah could mention changing her mind about identifying her secret admirer, he was striding toward the sales counter.

"We don't need the guy's address. We don't want his phone. You can hide his credit card number. All we want is a name,'' Matt was saying as Sarah joined him at the counter.

June riffled through the small box of index cards and receipts on the counter until she came to the one with Sarah's name and address on it. "Oh, sorry. He paid with cash.''

"So, that means what?'' Matt inquired.

"That we don't have a record of who sent the flowers. Just who they went to.''

Sarah touched Matt's sleeve. "That's okay.''

"No, it's not okay, Sarah. It means we've hit a dead end.''

"I know but…''

"No buts,'' Matt said. "Thank you for your time,'' he said to the women behind the counter. He caught Sarah's elbow and turned her toward the door, but June stopped him.

"Here's something interesting!'' she said, causing

Matt and Sarah to face her again. "The guy who sent the flowers also added a fifty-dollar tip for the delivery man."

"Fifty bucks?" Matt echoed incredulously.

That impressed even the college-student clerk. She snatched the slip from June and sighed. "Wow. Wish I would have made that delivery."

Equally curious, Sarah seized the slip from the clerk. She stared at the price of the flowers and the tip. "Money is obviously no object to this guy."

"No, it isn't," Matt said, then turned her toward the door and away from the eager ears of the florist shop staff. "And that worries me."

"We're back to the stalker theory again?" Sarah asked with a sigh as they walked out into the lowering light of late afternoon. If she lived to be 412 she would never understand Matt. He clearly liked her, yet he was helping her look for her secret admirer, even as he took every opportunity to disparage the poor guy.

"We can't get away from that."

"Sure we can."

"No, we can't! Throwing money around for no good reason is irresponsible, reckless—unless he's doing it to lure you in!"

"Did you ever stop to think," Sarah asked, getting angry now, because the worst of it was that he didn't realize that his continual objective analysis of the situation might be insulting to her, "that the reason the guy was willing to spend so much money and even leave a generous tip is because he has some cash? Is it so far-fetched to think that somebody with money likes me?"

"No! I didn't mean to insult you."

"Well, you did," Sarah said and pivoted away from him.

"Okay. Come on. I'm sorry."

Sarah marched away. "I don't care. I'm tired of you today. I want to go home."

"But I promised you dinner," Matt called running to catch her.

Though she refused to look at him, Sarah said, "I'll eat a tomato."

"A tomato is not a balanced meal."

"That might be true, but eating with somebody who makes me mad isn't good for digestion."

"If I promise not to make you mad anymore, will you let me buy you dinner?"

She sighed. There was no point in arguing with Matt. If she didn't give in now, he'd badger her until he wore her down. She might as well quit arguing and save them both some trouble. "All right. But don't expect me to talk to you."

Matt didn't know how it happened, but as they were seated at the restaurant, he knew the tables had been officially turned. She had shifted their situation from her being defensive about the fact that her secret admirer could be a stalker, to him being defensive about the fact that he seemed to keep insulting her. They ate their meal in almost complete silence. Not wanting to take her home while she was still upset with him, Matt talked her into dessert. Unfortunately, sugar seemed to get her going again.

"For all you know, the secret admirer could be Grant Lawson."

Matt almost spat out his coffee. He had thought exactly the same thing.

"Or Brett Hamilton."

He hadn't considered that the secret admirer might

be Brett, but he didn't like thinking about the suave British expatriate with Sarah any more than he liked imagining her with Wintersoft's handsome legal counsel. "I'm not saying…"

"Or Jack Devon."

Matt smiled. This wasn't Devon's style.

"Or Reed Connors."

That made him frown. Reed Connors was a normal guy. A handsome, successful guy, who would be a wonderful match for Sarah.

"Or even Nate Leeman."

Thank God. Somebody he could argue against. "Nate is too much of a loner…"

"See, there you go again!"

"What? I'm just saying that Nate's perfect mate would have to fall into his lap because he isn't the kind of guy to court a woman."

"Unlike you, Mr. Romance," Sarah said, then rose from her seat. "The closest you've ever gotten to even being nice was to say I reminded you of an exotic flower and I'm not a hundred percent sure you meant that. I'm not even a hundred percent sure you actually realize what you said."

She headed for the door, and Matt grabbed the check and followed her, sorting through the necessary cash as he ran in order to save time. "I don't need change," he told the cashier, then hustled out into the street to catch Sarah.

"Nate *is* unlike me!" Matt said, when he reached her.

Sarah said, "Whatever," and took a seat on the bench at the bus stop.

Matt gaped at her. "Oh, come on. Don't tell me you're not going to let me drive you home."

"I'm not going to let you drive me home."

"Just because I counted out one of Wintersoft's bachelors?"

"You counted everybody out."

"No, I didn't! In fact, in my head, I decided Reed Connors was a perfect candidate to be your stalker."

"Very funny."

"All right. The truth is, in my head I decided Reed Connors is the perfect match for you."

She brightened immediately. "Really?"

"Yeah," Matt said, but he deflated in direct proportion to the amount she brightened, because that meant she liked Reed. Still, rather than try to argue her out of that opinion, Matt let it go. The truth was he was going to have to get accustomed to her dating someone someday, because he wasn't allowed to pursue her. He might as well start now.

He drew a quiet breath. "Yeah. I think you two would make a nice couple. So, come on. Let me drive you home."

Sarah smiled and rose from the bench, walking with him to the parking garage and his car.

"I like Reed."

Unlocking his car door, Matt said, "I do, too."

"He's brainy, but not too. You know, he's brainy in the attractive kind of way."

"Right."

"And his family is normal."

"So is mine. You met my dad at the little Christmas party I had at his house last year. He's about as normal as a guy gets. My parents might be divorced, but he raised me just like any other kid."

She peered at him after she buckled her seat belt. "I

might have met your dad, but you never told me much about your situation.''

''There isn't much to tell. My mother left us when I was ten. My dad's a CPA.''

Sarah smiled. ''Like you.''

Matt maneuvered his car out of the parking garage. ''Actually, I took after him. He was a great role model.'' He pulled the car into the slow traffic of a lazy Saturday night and merged into the lane he needed. ''He taught me about goals and positive expectations, hard work and staying on track.''

''From the laughing I did with him at your party I never would have thought he was the one to blame for your being such a stick-in-the-mud.''

''I'm not a stick-in-the-mud!''

''Sure you are. Not only are you intent on pointing out something wrong with every potential secret admirer, but also you're just plain obsessed with your goals and life plan. I can't remember the last time you talked about going out simply to have fun and it seems like to you, everything relates back to money somehow.''

Matt hazarded a glance in her direction. ''You've never been poor, have you?''

''My family's not rich…''

''But you've never done without.''

She grimaced, almost feeling ashamed to admit it. ''No.''

''And you have some kind of money source other than work, or you wouldn't have had the cash to finance your recent makeover.''

''Inheritance from my grandmother.''

''I figured.''

''It's not a crime.''

"No, but it does keep you from understanding things that I've lived."

Sarah couldn't argue that. Mostly because she wasn't sure what he'd lived. She peeked at him. "So what went wrong in your life that caused you to focus on money?"

He scowled. "I'm not focused on money."

"If you're intimating that my family's good financial standing prevented me from worrying about money, then that has to mean that something about yours shifted your focus to it."

He sighed. "Did you ever stop to think that the reason our focus is different is simply because we're opposites?"

"About money?"

"No, about everything. You're comfortable and happy and can easily accept what life hands you. You even like surprises. You're one of those 'make lemonade out of lemons' people. I don't like not knowing what's coming next. If I get lemons I might make lemonade, but you better believe I'll be preparing for lemons next time around and won't get surprised." He paused to sigh. "So we're opposites. Which means there's no reason for us to argue anymore."

"What you're really saying is that our being opposites gives us a way out of this discussion without either one of us having to be wrong."

"Yes."

She thought about that for a few seconds and decided he was right. "Okay, then we're opposites."

Matt laughed. "Good." He pulled his car into a parking space in her apartment complex. "I'll walk you to your door."

"I'm fine!"

"See," he said. "Here's a perfect example of our

differences right here. You believe the best about your secret admirer, but I see the negative possibilities. Not because I'm negative, but because I'm cautious.''

She unbuckled her seat belt. ''You're not calling me flighty, are you?''

''No, I just think you're very trusting. And until you're sure this guy isn't a stalker it might not hurt to take my advice.''

She sighed heavily, but didn't argue. Instead, she got out of his car and said nothing as they strode to the building and while they rode the elevator to her floor.

When they reached her door, she faced him. ''Thanks for coming with me today.''

''You're welcome,'' he said, then noticed that her hair caught the light in the corridor and reflected it back. For the first time in a long time Matt felt perfectly comfortable and he recognized it was because they had admitted they were opposites. More than that, she had accepted that they could be different without one of them being wrong. She had let him be right, because he was right. Her good looks and sex appeal might bring him to his knees, and her innate goodness and kindness might make him long to be able to pursue her. But their being boss and assistant was only the tip of the iceberg of why they couldn't be together. The real culprit was that they were opposites. That was why he had told his dad he wouldn't ask her to transfer out of his department. It would be pointless to lose a good assistant so that they could try a relationship that he knew in his heart wouldn't work.

''Well, goodnight,'' Sarah said, smiling up at him.

Matt felt the tingle of desire shiver through him, but he knew it wasn't appropriate to follow through. At the same time, it didn't seem right just to walk away, either.

They'd reached a level of trust with their admission about being opposites, and though they couldn't get married, sleep together or even date, he didn't think one kiss goodnight—a kiss to seal their mutual *regret* that they didn't belong together—would really hurt anything.

He set his hands on her shoulders, lowered his head and brushed his lips across hers, feeling a hundred things he hadn't felt in the first, rushed, spontaneous kiss. He meant this. He wasn't operating on instinct or hormones. He fully intended to kiss her this time to let her know he liked her. And it felt wonderful.

It felt so wonderful that he slid his hands from her shoulders, down her back. Taking note of the fact that she wasn't arguing or fighting the kiss, Matt deepened it. He rubbed his lips across hers, enjoying the sensation of being so close, so intimate, and then nudged her mouth open with a small push from his tongue. When she accommodated him, a thousand shooting stars exploded in his brain and Matt felt things he had never believed he could.

The warmth of acceptance tangled with the power of sexual attraction, and he knew he could have taken her right there, on the threshold of her apartment. Desire and need tumbled through him, and he could feel, in her response to his deep, passionate kiss, that Sarah felt them too. But realizing she felt the same way he did actually cleared his head and got him to step back.

"Don't settle for a secret admirer or for trying to make something work that shouldn't," he said, staring into her pretty green eyes. "Wait for the right guy. The guy you deserve. The guy who deserves you."

With that he turned and began walking to the elevator, feeling empty and miserable, even though he knew he was doing the right thing.

Chapter Six

Monday morning, Sarah strode to Carmella's office rather than into her own. Carmella instantly glanced up and greeted her with a big smile. "Sarah, good morning! How are you?"

"Fine."

"Did you and Matt have any luck finding your secret admirer this weekend?"

"No. That's actually why I'm here."

Carmella motioned for Sarah to take the seat in front of her desk. "What's up?"

"The person who sent me flowers didn't leave his name because he didn't have to. He paid with cash. I think the florist shop is a dead end. So I'm back for more advice."

"I don't have any. Those flowers were our only link to the guy." Carmella caught her gaze. "Besides, I thought after this weekend, you wouldn't need any more advice. I kind of thought you and Matt might hit it off."

"He doesn't like me, Carmella," Sarah said, then

shook her head. It hurt her heart to say that aloud, especially since it wasn't precisely true. So she amended her answer to the real reason why the man she adored didn't want her.

"Well, he does like me. He all but admitted it at the florist's shop. But we're opposites. He kissed me then told me I shouldn't have to chase secret admirers or fight to make something work that doesn't and told me to wait for the right guy."

Carmella smiled knowingly. "He still kissed you."

"Yeah, but only to seal the deal that we're not good for each other."

"Well, that doesn't make sense. Particularly since that's the second time he's kissed you. He's got to have some feelings for you."

"He does. He told me that I was exotic and beautiful and I could see in his eyes that he meant it, but he doesn't want to have feelings for me. I get the sense that's because they make him behave in ways he can't control." She sighed heavily. "Let's face it, Carmella, the only time he does anything even halfway romantic is when the secret admirer does something. It's as if he can't help himself."

Carmella appeared to be pondering that. "You know what? I think you're right."

"I know I'm right." Sarah paused, then said, "So you don't have any advice for me about finding my secret admirer?"

"I'm afraid I'm fresh out."

"That means Matt doesn't want me and I can't find my secret admirer. I'm sunk."

As she turned away from Carmella's desk, Sarah saw Nelson O'Connor, one of the supervisors in the customer troubleshooting division. Tall and wiry, with unkempt dark-brown hair and brown eyes hidden by thick glasses, he stood in the entryway to Carmella's office.

"Nelson!" Fear made Sarah's heart clench when she realized he could have been standing there long enough to hear the pathetic description of her life.

"Hi, Sarah."

Knowing she had only one recourse in this situation, Sarah said, "Nelson, I don't know how much of that conversation you heard, but I would appreciate it if you kept it confidential."

Nelson made a cross over his pocket protector. "No one will hear it from me."

"Good," Sarah said, walking out of Carmella's office and down the hall to her workstation.

Now it was official. She was pathetic. Someone had caught her admitting she was desperate enough to look for her secret admirer. She couldn't go on embarrassing herself like this, so this had to be the end of all of it. Matt didn't like her and the secret admirer didn't want to be found.

The delivery person arrived at a quarter after eleven. But this man didn't have flowers. He had candy. An enormous box of chewy chocolate delights. Sarah stared at them.

"What do you think it means?" Penny said as she also stared at the ten-pound box.

Sarah said, "Well, for one thing, the guy obviously doesn't mind if I gain weight."

Penny giggled.

"For another, he might know that I've been to the florist's shop."

"Oh," Penny said, thinking that through. "He

doesn't want you to find out who he is so he switched stores."

"Or he knows I won't go back to the florist's shop because I know it's a dead end, so he's sending me to a new store, where he might have left his name."

"Or where the clerk might know his name," Penny speculated.

"Or where the clerk would pay enough attention that she could give a good description," Carmella suggested, walking to Sarah's desk. She stopped beside Penny. "Mr. Winters is here," she reminded the receptionist. "And he warned all of us about spending too much time at Sarah's desk."

"Yes, ma'am," Penny said and scampered up the hall.

Carmella faced Sarah. "Nice gift."

"Yeah. I like this one the best because I can't eat flowers, but I can drown my sorrows in this chocolate. Want a piece?"

"No. I just came down to send Penny back to her desk before Lloyd noticed she was missing," Carmella said with a laugh, then turned to return to her workstation.

Leaving the box of chocolates in plain sight so that anyone passing by would feel free to help themselves, Sarah went back to work, too.

Five minutes later, Matt came out of his office. "What's that?" he asked as he dropped a near-final draft of the quarterly report on her desk.

Sarah peeked up. "Candy."

He sighed. "I guess I don't have to ask who it's from."

"Since he doesn't sign his name, I wouldn't be able to tell you anyway."

Matt scowled "Right."

"Come on, Matt. You can't think bad thoughts about a guy who sends candy. If nothing else, the gift proves he's good-natured. Sending candy is like saying he doesn't mind if I gain weight."

"Or he's trying to get you to trust him. Stalkers don't start off being mean. They start by sending gifts, gaining your trust…"

"Hey!"

Sarah spun her chair around to see Nelson O'Connor striding down the hall. He pushed his glasses up his nose before he stopped at her desk. "Penny said you got candy."

"Yeah," Sarah said, glancing uneasily at Matt. She knew he didn't dislike her secret admirer only because he thought the guy could be a stalker. Matt also hated the disruption of their work time. His scowl of disapproval confirmed that.

Nelson seemed oblivious. "You don't sound like the candy cheered you up."

"Oh, it did, Nelson," Sarah said quickly, not just trying to get him to go back to his own office, but also not wanting him to talk about her conversation with Carmella in front of Matt. Remembering that Nelson had heard her pathetic remarks, she realized it was a tad coincidental that she had gotten candy after he had been exposed to her troubles. In fact, it made her wonder if the shift from flowers to candy didn't result from a change in gift-sender. Wanting to lift her spirits, Nelson could very well have sent this box of candy.

"Good, because I'm sure that's what the guy wanted to do. Cheer you up."

Sarah decided that that comment was even more evidence that Nelson might have sent her this candy, but before she could say anything, Matt pushed away from his doorframe. "You know, Nelson, I'm glad you're here."

Nelson brightened. "Really?"

"Yeah. Sarah and I sort of have a disagreement about her secret admirer and I just realized that what we need is an objective opinion."

Nelson swallowed. "Oh, don't ask me about personal stuff," he began, but Matt interrupted him.

"You're allowed to have an opinion, Nelson. And really, that's all this is right now, because we don't have any facts. So we're just trying to figure this out based on opinion. For instance, I think there's a reason the secret admirer is remaining anonymous."

Nelson drew a quick breath. "Yes. I would have to agree with that."

"And that makes him dangerous."

Nelson looked shocked. "What? How could sending a gift make somebody dangerous? *Nice* people send gifts."

Matt shook his head. "It isn't the gifts that trouble me. It's the way he sends them. A normal, healthy man wouldn't send gifts anonymously. He would want credit."

Nelson backed away from Sarah's desk. "I don't know. I don't think so. When someone sends a gift from the heart he doesn't need credit."

Ariana appeared, walking down the hall toward Sarah's workstation. "Hey, I heard somebody back here has candy."

"I do, Ariana," Sarah said.

"I better get going!" Nelson said and scrambled away.

Obviously disturbed by yet another interruption, Matt shook his head and retreated into his office.

But Sarah was fuming. Not just because Matt couldn't let the secret-admirer-stalker theory go, but because he had scared the wits out of poor Nelson. And he didn't even seem to realize that he had!

As soon as Ariana left, Sarah had every intention of talking to him, but she couldn't because Sunny returned from her break and then a steady stream of secretaries stole back to Sarah's workstation not only to see the candy, but also to eat a piece. It was ten after twelve before she could go into Matt's office.

"That was just mean!"

Matt looked up from his work. "What was mean? Walking out of your office because I didn't care to see the fifty people who would stop by your desk, take a piece of candy and keep you from working for the past hour?"

"No," Sarah said, understanding he had every right to be disturbed about that. "I'm talking about Nelson. Don't you see that you insulted him! Sending a gift anonymously is exactly what somebody like Nelson would do!"

Matt leaned back in his chair. "And don't you see that was exactly my point?"

"What point!"

"That your secret admirer might not be a stalker, but he probably isn't Grant Lawson either. There's a reason this guy isn't signing his name."

"Do you think I don't know that!"

"I think you know it, but I think you're choosing to ignore it." He tossed his pencil to his desk and sighed. "There's a part of me that's afraid for you."

"I know. Because I'm too trusting. But it's not always a bad thing to trust…"

"It's not always a good thing to trust, either."

"You know what, Matt? I think the real issue here is that you can't trust at all."

"When did this become about me?"

"The minute you decided to be my guardian or conscience or whatever you seem to think you have a right to be about the secret admirer."

"This isn't about me."

"As long as you think you have a right to make comments every time I get a gift, then I'm going to think it's my right to make assumptions about you. And right now I have to ask why it is that you can't just accept that somebody would be kind enough to send a gift."

"Because there's always a reason people do what they do."

Sarah shook her head sadly. "If that's how you really feel, how you really see life, I feel sorry for you," Sarah said and walked out of his office just in time to spot Lloyd Winters striding down the hall.

"Hi, Mr. Winters," she said, grabbing her jacket and purse.

Lloyd stopped beside her desk. "Going to lunch?"

"Yes."

"I want to see you when you get back."

"Okay," Sarah said, realizing that he'd probably noticed the steady stream of congratulators seeking a piece of her candy and that she was probably going to get an official reprimand.

She stormed out of the building, fuming that this situation had been blown out of proportion and it was time to get it under control again. Knowing that she could prove her point about the candy being a kind gesture simply by proving that Nelson had sent it, Sarah turned in the direction of the gift shop that had delivered the candy and walked the two blocks to its door. When she opened it, an overhead bell jingled and a clerk came out of the door behind the counter to greet her.

"Hi! What can I do for you?"

"I got a box of candy this morning. I need to know who sent it."

The short, balding man sighed. "You're not here to buy something?"

"No, I just need…"

The clerk shook his head. "Time is money, kid, and I am just about broke. I invested everything I had into this shop and it's not taking off the way it should. I'm not wasting my time or my energy talking to people who aren't buying."

"Okay, I'll buy something," she said, then inspiration stuck. "I'll take a ten-pound box of candy just like the one delivered to me this morning."

"I delivered three boxes of candy this morning. You have to be more specific."

"How about this? Give me the same kind of candy you delivered to Sarah Morris this morning."

The clerk sighed. "I take it you're Sarah Morris."

Sarah only smiled.

"Well, that's one way to do this," the clerk said and punched a few keys on his computer screen. "You got the deluxe assortment." He paused and chuckled. "Are you also going to give me the fifty-dollar tip?"

"This isn't delivery. It's takeout, remember?"

"My loss," the clerk said with a shrug. "That'll be two hundred dollars."

Sarah gaped at him. "Two hundred dollars!"

"The chocolate's imported."

"For that price it should sing to me while I type."

The clerk laughed. "Good one."

"Right," Sarah said, then handed him her credit card. He put the card through the machine, it was approved and he handed her the slip to sign.

"Okay, now can I have the name of the guy who sent the other box to me?"

The clerk hit two buttons and the screen changed. "Oh, sorry. He paid with cash."

"What!" Sarah said, scampering around the counter to look at the screen. "Damn it! You could have told me that."

"I didn't know that from the first screen." He smiled. "You should have told me to check if it was a cash sale before you bought your box."

Sarah groaned. "Right. Can you at least tell me what the guy looked like?"

"I can't even tell you if it was a guy. Whoever it was came in while my wife was manning the store while I was at the dentist." His regretful smile almost looked sincere. "By the way, did I mention we have a no-refund policy?"

"No, but it doesn't surprise me." Sarah headed for the door, but returned to the counter and grabbed her two-hundred-dollar box of chocolates. She slammed out the door and marched up the street to the office again. She would be damned if this secret admirer wouldn't be the death of her—or at the very least the death of her inheritance from her grandmother.

Matt worked twenty minutes into his lunch hour before he realized he had to end this secret-admirer thing once and for all. If Sarah was right, if the secret admirer had sent her candy to give her a fresh lead, then Matt wasn't going to wait around for the weekend. He was going to take the lead, find this guy and prove to Sarah that she should drop her interest in him and maybe even refuse any more deliveries.

He got the address for the gift shop from the card for the box of candy that Sarah had left in plain sight on her desk. He walked out of the building and down the street to the gift shop, which was so close he had the uncomfortable feeling Sarah's secret admirer had to be someone who worked for Wintersoft.

"Hi, I'm Matt Burke," he said to the middle-aged man behind the counter. "Can you tell me who you sold a ten-pound deluxe assortment box of chocolates to recently?"

The clerk, a middle-aged man with sagging muscles and a severe scowl, took in Matt's size, and apparently made the decision to comply based on the fact that they both knew Matt could easily whip him in a fight.

"Yeah, I sold a box to a..." he riffled through a stack of credit-card receipts. "Sarah Morris."

Matt resisted the urge to grab the slip to make the confirmation. "You're sure? Sarah Morris?"

"Yeah. I'm sure," the clerk singsonged as if annoyed.

Matt began backing out of the gift shop to the door. "Okay," he said, then pushed his way into the street.

Sarah had sent her own damned candy.

It was highly possible she'd also sent the flowers.

She could be her own damned secret admirer.

The question was...why?

Matt started adding things up in his head. He didn't consider Sarah to be a devious person, but she *was* an inventive person. She had told him she'd had a crush on him most of the year they'd worked together. She got angry any time he insulted her secret admirer. And she had very cleverly used the secret admirer to get them together outside the office and even to get him to talk about his personal life. He'd told her about his dad and this morning she'd used his mistrust of the gift-giver's motives to get him almost to talk about his inability to trust people.

She was either very desperate or very clever, and for two minutes Matt was complimented both by the fact that she could like him enough to implement such a bold strategy and by the fact that she was willing to go so far to capture his attention. But in the end, he decided that it didn't matter. He wasn't ready to get married and they were too different. A relationship between them would never work. There was no sense dabbling in or wishing for the impossible.

When he arrived at the office, he stopped at her desk. "You and I need to talk."

She sighed. "Matt, I'm having the worst day of my life. Can we save it for tomorrow?"

"No, I want to get this out in the open now."

He motioned for her to precede him into his office and Sarah did, but not without a long-suffering sigh.

"All right," she said as Matt closed his door. "What's this all about?"

"I went to the gift shop today. I know you sent yourself that candy."

She gaped at him. "What?"

"I went to the gift shop," Matt repeated slowly, feeling like hell. For as much as he wanted this whole mess to settle down, he couldn't stop the thought that she cared enough about him to go to such lengths to get his attention and here he was reprimanding her.

Yet, he had to stop this. The gifts couldn't continue. The ruse wasn't right.

"The clerk told me the person who bought the ten-pound box of candy this morning was Sarah Morris."

Sarah dropped her head to her hands. "This day cannot get any worse." She blew her breath out on a long sigh and raised her head to look at him again. "Matt, the only way I could get that clerk to talk to me was if I bought a box of candy. I bought the same kind of candy sent to me so that he could get into the records."

"Sarah, I understand that you're embarrassed..."

"I'm not embarrassed! And I'll prove it," she said, jumping from the chair and storming to the door, which she yanked open. Thirty seconds later she dropped two boxes of candy on his desk with a loud thud. "See, I was trying to get information, just like you were!"

"You know, you two are just the berries."

The comment came from Lloyd Winters; both Sarah and Matt froze.

"You're two of the smartest people in the building," he said, strolling into the room. "Yet you're letting some anonymous stranger screw up a working relationship that has been above reproach for the past year."

Matt drew a slow breath. "I'm sorry, Lloyd. This is my fault."

"No, Matt, it's not your fault."

"You're right, Mr. Winters," Sarah jumped in immediately. "It's mine."

Lloyd smiled at her. "It's not yours, either, Sarah. This mess is the fault of your secret admirer. However," he added, stopping beside Matt's desk. "Neither of you seems to know how to deal with this. So," he said as he reached into his jacket pocket and pulled out two envelopes. "I had Carmella search the Internet and she found a seminar on interpersonal skills in the work-place."

Matt groaned. Wide-eyed, Sarah only stared at Lloyd.

"It's in New Hampshire. Only about an hour and a half away. You can drive up together, learn to deal with this problem, have a nice dinner on Wintersoft, and then come home refreshed and able to deal with this."

"But we…"

"Have a quarterly statement due?" Lloyd said, finishing Matt's question.

Matt nodded.

"I just reviewed the most recent version and put it on Sarah's desk. Once she inputs my corrections, it's done. You two don't have another deadline for a couple of weeks. You can spare a day out of the office." He paused, shook his head, then said, "You two *need* a day out of the office."

Chapter Seven

"I did not *need* a day out of the office," Matt groused as he and Sarah walked away from the registration desk for the seminar. "And no matter what Lloyd says, I can't afford a day away."

Sarah tried to ignore her boss by pretending great interest in entering the hotel meeting room housing their class. But when she saw the ten tables in two rows down the center of the room, she almost groaned. Covered with white linen cloths and sporting water bottles—even with the complimentary pens and paper at each place— the tables looked more like a setup for a dining room than a classroom. She knew that the casual setting was not going to please the man who lived for professionalism, business ethics and order.

She knew she was right when Matt sighed. "Lloyd couldn't pick something sponsored by a university. No, he sends us to an infomercial waiting to happen."

Sarah faced her surly companion. "This isn't an infomercial. The group giving this seminar is reputable."

"Then why aren't they at a university?"

"I don't know. Maybe they draw better crowds at hotels," Sarah said, heading for the farthest row of tables, carrying the workbook she'd received when she and Matt registered.

Matt stopped abruptly. "You want to sit in the back of the room?"

"You want to sit in the front?"

"Yes. If I have to be here, I at least want to hear the speaker."

"Fine." She didn't bother telling Matt that she'd been to these kinds of seminars before and sitting in the front was a clue to the speaker that you wanted to participate. After listening to him complain for over an hour, she thought it poetic justice that his seat choice would make him a very active participant in the seminar he didn't want to have to attend.

She followed him to the first row of tables and took a seat beside his, then wondered how she would survive another six hours in his company. Not only was he unhappy about spending a day out of the office, but also she was still miffed at him for scaring Nelson and angrier still that he accused her of being her own secret admirer.

By the time she realized that she didn't need to sit with Matt just because they worked together, the speaker was bounding enthusiastically to the podium.

"Good morning!" he bellowed. "I'm your host Rod Jamison." Short and stocky, dressed in an expensive black suit and savvy aqua tie, Rod Jamison exuded the kind of confidence that Sarah appreciated in anyone.

He took the microphone from the holder on the podium beside the overhead projector, and strode down the aisle separating the two rows of tables until he stood in the exact center of the crowd of attendees.

"We're going to start things off by playing a little game. Does everybody like games?"

An enthusiastic "Yeah!" erupted from the crowd.

Matt squeezed his eyes shut. "Dear God."

Sarah ignored him and focused on Rod.

"The first game is simple. I want you to introduce yourself to the people on each side of you. Include where you work in your introduction, then tell that person something personal about yourself." He laughed. "Not something naughty! This isn't that kind of seminar," he added with a wink. "Just something like your favorite color or your favorite time of year, to give your classmate a feel for your personality."

He glanced at his watch. "You have thirty seconds…go!"

Continuing to avoid Matt, Sarah turned to the woman beside her. "I'm Sarah Morris. I work for Wintersoft. And my favorite color is green."

"I'm Janice Replogle. I work for this hotel, believe it or not," the tall brunette said with a laugh. "And I still sleep with a teddy bear."

"Me too!" Sarah said, but Matt tapped her on the shoulder.

When she faced him he said, "If I'm here, I'm doing everything he says. So, I'm Matt Burke, I work for Wintersoft, and my favorite color is blue."

Because she knew coming to this seminar was absolute torture for her stiff and stoic boss, yet he had decided to be a good sport about it, Sarah smiled supportively. After all, as his executive assistant, it was her job to support the guy.

Sarah also admitted to herself that she hadn't exactly

been treating Matt like a boss lately. When she thought about their professional roles, she realized she would have to forget her anger over Matt scaring Nelson and insulting her, because both were irrelevant to their boss/assistant relationship. Particularly since they still had to work together. That was why they were here, and if she, like Matt, intended to follow Lloyd's orders and learn to get along, then she had to participate, too.

"I'm Sarah Morris, I work for Wintersoft and my favorite season is fall."

"Really?"

"Yeah. I love fall. I love the trees. I love crisp air. I love the unpredictability of it."

Matt studied her for a second. "I didn't know that. After all the time we've worked together and since we're in that season right now, it seems odd that I never picked up on that."

"Don't worry about it," Sarah said with a laugh. "I didn't know you liked blue."

"It's hard not to like blue. It's a universal favorite."

"I guess," Sarah said, as the strangest feeling stole through her. If she didn't know his favorite color and he didn't know her favorite season, then there was another conclusion to be drawn. They really didn't know much about each other. And Matt really didn't want to find out any more or take their relationship any further. So, this was it. Boss and assistant were probably all they would ever be to each other.

"I'm sorry I was so grouchy this morning."

She stared into his eyes, and let the realization sink in that they would never fall in love, never be lovers. The notion filled her with regret, but honesty with herself compelled her to acknowledge it was probably for the best. Especially since nothing had happened between them and they could easily go back to being comfortable with each other in their work roles.

She cleared her throat and said, "Yeah, I'm sorry you were so grouchy this morning, too."

Matt smiled, and something inside Sarah wanted to weep. His sweet smile was one of the things she liked about him. As stuffy and stoic as Matt could be, he also had a soft side. She didn't see it often, but just as he claimed to have seen her feminine side, she had seen his soft side. And that was why she liked him. That was why she would always like him. Inside very serious, hard-working, play-by-the-rules Matt was a nice guy waiting to happen. But he didn't want her. He couldn't make it plainer. And it was time she accepted that.

"Okay!" Rod called. "Time's up! By now we should all feel comfortable with the people around us."

Sarah turned to face Rod again. Rod winked at her and every muscle in Matt's body stiffened, but he knew it was inappropriate to be jealous. Not just because he had no intention of pursuing Sarah, but because they had finally reached a truce of sorts. He'd jumped to all kinds of conclusions about her secret admirer that had gotten them into trouble, and it had taken until two minutes ago for her to speak civilly to him again. He couldn't be jumping to conclusions anymore, or, worse yet, deciding who could and couldn't be attracted to his assistant. When he did, he only made her angry, and when she was angry, she didn't hesitate to argue with him. And that was the reason they were at this ridiculous seminar in the first place.

At least that's what he'd let Sarah and probably everybody at Wintersoft believe, but Matt knew it was more than that. His real problem was that he liked Sarah. She tempted him to want things he had always known were wrong for him. That was why he was off balance. That was why he reacted so poorly. Inappropriate things had never tempted him before. They'd always been easy to resist. Sarah was not so easy to resist. She was definitely wrong for him. But she wasn't easy to resist.

Rod jogged to the front of the room again. "I would be a class-A dummy if I didn't realize all of you are here for a reason. If you begged to attend, that probably means there's a nasty person in your work life who rubs you the wrong way, and, civil, decent person that you are," he said, wiggling his eyebrows comically, "you're here to learn how to continue to be nice to him or her."

A chuckle rose from the crowd.

"But—and I hate to tell you this," Rod continued merrily. "If your coworkers, or worse, *your boss* sent you, my friend, you are in big trouble."

Matt mumbled, "No kidding."

"All right, now we're going to play another game. I'll tell you up-front that the point of this game is to see how honest you are."

Again, a chuckle rose from the crowd.

"I want everybody sent here by somebody else to raise his or her hand."

Matt didn't have to be a genius to realize that raising his hand right now would lead to serious embarrassment. Unfortunately, Sarah raised hers.

Rod clearly couldn't have been happier.

"My, my," he said, sashaying over to Sarah. "Pretty thing like you can't get along with her peers? I can't believe that."

Sarah laughed. "It's true. This guy right here," she said, angling her thumb at Matt, being the normally pleasant, open, happy woman she always was. "He's my boss and he's the one I can't seem to work with anymore. The owner of our company overheard us arguing and sent us here."

Rod laughed. "Well, now. That's quite a story. Care to add to that—" Rod paused to look at Matt's name tag "—Matt?"

"Not even a little bit."

"Ouch!" Rod said, then shifted away. "Okay, anybody else as honest as Sarah?"

"He knows your name."

"What?" Sarah asked, facing Matt.

"He didn't even glance at your name tag when he came over, yet he knows your name."

"He probably looked at it when we first came in."

"I'm sure he did."

"Okay! All right!" Rod yelled, striding from the back of the room to the front and stopping in front of Sarah and Matt. "I make it a rule never to share the floor. Care to tell the class what you're arguing about?"

Sarah cleared her throat. "It was stupid. Nothing anybody else would be interested in."

"But you were arguing."

"*Discussing* something," Matt clarified.

"Okay!" Rod said, happy again. "There are two good points in what Matt said, people."

He bounded to the center of the room. "Number one, don't call every disagreement an argument. Use creative vocabulary. Matt termed his conversation with Sarah a discussion, because that's what happens in business. If you don't agree with the guy in the next cubicle about where to put the telephone, you have to *discuss* it, because it's only through dialogue that you'll make the decision. Yet most of us would call that kind of interaction an argument. In other words, we set ourselves up for failure. And that takes us to our next game…''

Matt turned in his seat so he was fully facing Rod who still stood in the center of the room. "Wait. You said there were two points to what I said. You only gave us one of them.''

"Yes, I did, didn't I?" Rod said, once again scampering to stand in front of Sarah and Matt.

"So what's the second point?" Matt asked.

"The second point is that everything you say and do is being interpreted by the people around you. Your gestures, your tone of voice, the way you sit, stand and move all have meaning.''

"And you got that from what I said?''

"No, I got that from your tone, the set of your shoulders and the fact that you haven't smiled once since you arrived." He skipped away from Sarah and Matt to the center aisle again, but this time he stopped by the overhead protector by the podium in the front of the room.

"People, there are four types of personalities. There are rule-followers," he said, sliding a sheet onto the projector and producing a graphic that showed four quadrants.

"Rule-followers," he repeated, pointing at that block, "are people who need rules for everything. Semifollowers need lots of rules but can be flexible," he said pointing to the second block. "People who need some rules but are actually very flexible are the third type. And people who would throw out all the rules and live in the moment are the fourth.''

He strode to Matt and Sarah again. "You," he said, pointing at Matt, "are a rule-follower. You need rules and lots of them. To you that's how the world stays comfortable. And you," he said, pointing at Sarah, but also smiling flirtatiously, "would prefer that the rule book was dropped into the ocean. You're accommodating and generous, a hard worker who covers for others and a good listener."

"That's me exactly!" Sarah said with a gasp.

Matt scowled at the fact that she seemed so proud of herself and didn't see that being easygoing wasn't always the best route. That was why she kept giving her secret admirer the benefit of the doubt and why she might end up in serious trouble.

"Right, that is her exactly," Matt said, not wanting some seminar flunky to convince his assistant to continue searching for her secret admirer without even realizing he might be putting her in danger. "That's why we had fifty visitors a day when she started getting flowers from a secret admirer. And why I couldn't get any work done."

"Oh," Rod said, "this is getting interesting!"

"There's nothing interesting about it," Matt said, keeping the discussion in the realm of business so he wouldn't have to tell an entire room full of people that he was jealous of a man he didn't know, attracted to a woman he couldn't have and helpless to save her from God knew what. "Bottom line... We're here because she has nonstop visitors."

Sarah gasped. "Am I not getting my work done?"

"You're getting your work done," Matt said, ready to take his share of the blame and not force her to accept responsibility for something over which she had no control. "But I'm not. The noise and confusion distract me. I think you need to forget about your secret admirer and even start returning his gifts so he lets you alone."

"Okay, all this is good. Very healthy. Communication and all that," Rod said. "And though I'm not a therapist, I'm going to make the prediction right now that Sarah and Matt are the two people who will get the most out of this seminar because we can solve their problem. I'm going to teach you," he said, looking from Matt to Sarah and then back to Matt again, "to make your requests known without anger. Now," he added, skipping away again. "I'm not going to suggest that you go home and try using these techniques on your spouse!" He chuckled. "People from this quadrant," he said, pointing at the rule-follower block, "really don't belong with people from this quadrant." He pointed at the no-rules quadrant.

He smiled at Sarah and Matt. "As long as you two don't try to get romantically involved, we will fix all of your problems. But if you're thinking about getting involved, you will definitely need professional help."

The group broke into uproarious laughter and Matt knew Rod had only said that as a joke, but as the day wore on, two things became painfully clear. First, Rod might have hinted that they should stay away from each other romantically because he wanted Sarah for himself. Second, Sarah believed every darned word the guy said. Matt knew that because she hung on his every syllable, chose to eat lunch with him and hugged him goodbye.

Matt wasn't surprised it was raining when they left the hotel. He knew the remnants of a hurricane were scheduled to pass through the northeast. But having water beat against them as they ran to his car didn't help Matt's mood. He felt trapped. He couldn't dislike Sarah because she was likable, but he couldn't have her because they weren't right for each other. Even goofy Rod had seen that. Yet he was doomed to be in her company, watching other guys fall all over themselves to get her attention and knowing that ultimately one of them was going to succeed.

"Well, that was fun."

"A real laugh riot," Matt said, backing his car out of the hotel parking lot. Rain pummeled the windshield and roof so loudly it created an echo in the car.

"Come on, once we settled in and Rod stopped calling on us, I thought even you had fun."

"I did what I had to do."

She smiled dreamily. "That's right. Rule-follower."

At her undying devotion to short, snappy Rod, Matt wanted to puke. But he didn't. He wouldn't. As Rod had said, the best way for him and Sarah to get along would be to avoid a personal connection and function purely as business associates. "Precisely."

Sarah stole a quick peek at Matt, then looked out the car window again. Because he didn't argue with her but answered only as her boss would answer, Sarah knew the seminar had been a success. They were back to being boss and assistant again. She got comfortable in her seat and closed her eyes because she didn't want to push things by continuing the conversation. But the intensity of the rain beating on the car roof scared her. She knew the storm was the unpredictable remnants of yet another hurricane, and, after a few minutes of trying to pretend it didn't frighten her, she faced Matt again to distract herself.

"At least you had to like Rod."

"He was good with the crowd, and he got through the entire workbook. So, he was a good teacher."

"And a great guy."

"Frankly, I thought he was a tad overenthusiastic."

Matt pulled the car onto the highway and merged into the slow-moving traffic. Sarah cast a worried eye at the rain pummeling the pavement on the road in front of them, and, though she recognized Rod probably wasn't the best topic of conversation, talking about him was at least better than watching the storm.

"I think seminar speakers are supposed to be over-enthusiastic."

"Then Rod was an ace."

Her fear over the slicing rain only compounded her annoyance over Matt's refusal to be nice about Rod, and Sarah concluded it would be better to keep to herself for the drive. But as the minutes passed, the rain grew stronger, her nerves jangled, and she could hardly sit still, let alone stay quiet.

"I'm a competent driver."

"I didn't say you weren't."

Matt laughed. "Your body language is saying it."

The little dig didn't help Sarah's disposition. "Get that from Rod?"

"As a matter of fact, yes," Matt said with a brief chuckle, but his laughter ended when the car jerked unexpectedly. "Damn it! There's so much water on the road, I'm hydroplaning."

"Oh, good," Sarah said. Her hands fisted tightly and her knuckles whitened. "At least we only have another hour on the road."

Matt peered at her. "Actually, it might not be a good idea to stay on the road."

"You think we should pull over?"

He shook his head. "I think we need to do more than pull over. We should find a hotel. This is the end of a hurricane. It will last for hours, probably through most of the night. The easiest thing to do would be take the next exit and look for a room."

"You won't get an argument out of me."

"Then that would be a first."

Sarah said nothing as Matt eased his vehicle off the highway and down the exit ramp. They turned left, toward the bank of hotels and Sarah immediately noticed the parking lot of the first one was full.

"No point in stopping there."

Matt quietly said, "No. I think you're right. It's full. Besides there are three more hotels along this stretch of road."

They pulled into the next one and both ran to the lobby. A long line of potential guests stood at the counter.

"We can wait here and maybe not get a room," Matt said, glancing at Sarah. "Or we can try the next one."

"We might as well go to the next one," Sarah said, then dashed out into the rain again.

At the third hotel they waited behind six customers who took the last available rooms. So at the final hotel when the clerk said there was only one room available, Sarah didn't hesitate. "We'll take it."

Matt faced her. "Oh, really?"

"Yes, I'm afraid to drive in a storm this hard." Sarah reached for the key card. "Besides I'm sure the room has two double beds."

The clerk pulled the card back. "Sorry! This room has only one king-sized bed."

Sarah reached for the key again. "I'll sleep on the floor."

Matt took the key from her hands. "Sure, Rod would love that. He'd call me a stickler for comfort and you a sainted martyr. *I'll* sleep on the floor."

Chapter Eight

Throughout their dinner in the hotel restaurant Sarah stayed silent. Matt's shot about Rod violated their unspoken agreement to go back to being nothing more than coworkers, but Sarah had a sneaking suspicion Matt had gotten snippy about Rod because he was nervous. She was just about certain her assumption was correct when he suggested they stay in the hotel lounge and listen to the too-loud rock band rather than go back to their room.

One bed awaited two people. Two very sexually attracted people. Sarah had dismissed their sexual attraction that morning because it wasn't relevant in a work relationship. But when a man and a woman were stuck in a hotel room with only one bed, it became an issue again. Particularly since the attraction was so strong Sarah genuinely believed she and Matt would have fallen into a relationship by now if it weren't for the fact that Matt was so level-headed.

Still, Matt being level-headed could be part of the

problem. From her own parents, Sarah knew that an intense sexual attraction made people do crazy things. Her mother had traded living in the city to be with her husband, a rancher. Her dad had gone to parties he despised and learned to rub elbows with high society people to please his wife.

If her parents had been compelled to do things that they normally wouldn't have considered in response to love and sexual attraction, it wasn't far-fetched to think that *fighting* a sexual attraction would make Matt do even crazier things. It might not be in his life plan for him to like her, but he did, and as far as Sarah was concerned that was the real storm raging in Matt. He wanted her, but couldn't deal with it. And the end result was that their lives were a mess. He didn't want a relationship, but they couldn't work together anymore, either. Otherwise, he wouldn't have made that crack about Rod. He would have been able to control himself. If he didn't soon ask her to transfer out of his department, one or both of them would go insane. Unless, they went the opposite route and did something about the sexual attraction.

Walking back to the hotel room, Sarah actually wondered if the answer to this problem wouldn't be for her to seduce Matt and force him into a position where he had to deal with his feelings for her once and for all. It seemed like such a logical thing to do that Sarah had to wonder if fate hadn't led them here, on this day, in this storm, so she would get a chance to do exactly that.

When they entered their small hotel room Sarah looked around. One bed, two people. Was fate really trying to tell her something?

"You shower first."

Heart pumping, Sarah faced Matt. He was so handsome. Tall and broad-shouldered, with serious blue eyes and an adorable smile. Seducing him seemed so obvious, so easy, so logical. Once they made love, Matt wouldn't leave her, hurt her or desert her. He couldn't. He was too loyal and too responsible to leave a woman he'd made love to. Then they would have to work things out, learn to get along, learn to deal with each other's differences. Just as her parents had. And successfully, she might add.

Not wanting him to guess what she was thinking from the expression on her face, Sarah turned away. "There's not much point to a shower if I just have to put these old clothes back on."

"Don't forget I have my stuff from the car."

"*You* have *your* stuff from the car. I have nothing."

"Not true," he said, producing a duffel bag. "Not only do I keep jeans and a T-shirt in the trunk in case I have a flat tire, but I also have sweats and a T-shirt for the gym."

"I'm sure they smell great."

"I put fresh clothes in this bag after every workout."

"Right," Sarah said, back to debating again. Anybody who thought that far ahead and had that many extra clothes in his car had to be her polar opposite. She'd always known it, but until now she'd thought his overly cautious nature endearing. But coming head to head with their differences while thinking about seducing him made it all the more obvious, like an unwelcome warning beacon.

He tossed the sweats and T-shirt at her. "Shower and change into those. You'll feel much better."

Her eyes narrowed. Surely he wasn't blaming her for *his* inability to be civil? "Actually, I've been perfectly happy most of the day."

"And why not? You were the belle of the ball."

He said it as if she should be ashamed, and as if he had the right to be so cynical and critical, and Sarah made her quick choice. They were too different to have a relationship. It would be a cold, frosty day in hell before she seduced this guy.

After a relaxing shower and changing into the jeans and T-shirt he always carried in his car in case he got a flat, Matt finally felt like himself—and that meant he began to feel foolish. He stepped out of the bathroom and walked over to the bed, where Sarah lay sprawled on top of the comforter, dressed in the over-large sweats and T-shirt from his gym bag.

"I'm sorry that I'm so grouchy."

She didn't take her eyes off the television. "It's all right."

"No, it's not, or you would be able to look at me."

"I'm watching television."

"Okay. That's great," he said, because he knew he deserved any cold shoulder she wanted to give him. "But let's set a time limit, so we can both get some sleep."

"Sure. A time limit is exactly what we need. Any other rules you want to set up? We could put restrictions on the amount of light in the room, maybe set guidelines about phone usage."

"Very funny." He went to the closet, grabbed the two extra pillows and extra blanket and walked to the empty space between the bed and the round table with the lamp.

He tossed the blanket to the floor and realized it wouldn't give him much protection. "How many blankets are on the bed?"

"Why? You want to rip them in half to make sure we both get an even share?"

Matt sighed. "This isn't funny anymore, Sarah."

"You're right. It's not."

"All I'm trying to do is see if you'll have enough covers if I take the comforter and fold it to make something of a cushion between me and the floor."

This time Sarah sighed. "You're right. I'm sorry." She rose from the bed, pulled off the comforter and tossed it at him. "Here."

"Thanks," he said, folding it in half before he laid it on the floor. Though not precisely comfortable, his makeshift bed looked at least manageable. He lay down and arranged the blanket over himself, wishing he didn't have to sleep in jeans, but deciding that that was better than battling the driving rain for the hour or more it would take to get home. Or, worse, being naked in the same bed with a woman who drove him crazy with lust.

Sarah turned off the television and the lamp. From the sounds he heard above him, Matt knew she was settling in to go to sleep herself. Several minutes passed in strained silence. Finally she said, "Do you think our problem really is that we're opposites?"

Matt didn't hesitate. "Yes."

"You don't think it's jealousy or that we like each other but can't deal with it?"

Matt blew his breath out on a sigh. "Sarah, jealousy is a part of it. Any man would be attracted to you. But that's the point. *Any man* would be attracted to you. I'm a hundred percent normal in that regard. But I'm also smart enough to realize that it's wrong for us to make a relationship based only on a sexual attraction. If we had something else going for us, like, for instance, a hobby we shared, I might feel differently. But right now the only thing we've got is physical.'' He paused, drew a quiet breath and added, ''It's not enough.''

''So what you're saying is that Rod made a few valid points.''

Matt laughed. Though he hated agreeing with Rod, Rod was correct about Matt and Sarah. ''Yes. Rod's presentation did have a few valid points. He wasn't a complete lunkhead.''

''Actually, he was a really nice guy. We had a great lunch.''

''Good.''

''And I feel really stupid up here.'' Sarah sighed. ''Matt, the bed is a king-sized bed. It's huge. I'm wearing clothes way too big for me. You have jeans on. Even if we accidentally bumped into each other, we're so cushioned we probably wouldn't feel it.''

Matt squeezed his eyes shut. That was typical Sarah. He had just told her he was sexually attracted to her, but in her usual cavalier way, she had dismissed it. However, maybe in this case she hadn't dismissed it because she didn't think it important. Maybe she'd dismissed it because his rational response to her question about Rod proved he intended to be reasonable about this. Maybe she wanted to be fair and share the bed. Because the bed *was* big. And because it really wasn't right for one of them to be uncomfortable when there was so much space available.

Not only was she correct, but she had just reminded him there was another thing to like about her aside from her great looks. She was generous. Actually, she was generous, kind and fair.

''All right. You're right,'' he said, and unrolled himself from the floor.

Sarah turned on a lamp and Matt tossed the extra

pillows back in the closet, then grabbed the comforter and blanket and took them to the bed. "But we don't share covers. The way I have this figured, if we use different blankets, there's little chance we'll roll into each other."

Sarah nodded. "Makes sense."

"Good."

"Good."

Sarah yanked her covers to her side of the bed. When she was settled, Matt sat cautiously.

"Get the light," she instructed, rolling to face the side opposite him.

Matt looked at the bed then looked at the nice curve of her bottom, which rested a good foot from the side of the bed he would inhabit. He suppressed a sigh of longing, but knew all this was for the best. She was generous, kind and fair, and he was a gentleman. They shouldn't have a problem.

He flicked off the lamp and lay down. Hands behind his head, he stared out into the darkness and his conscience began to bother him. With all this fairness rolling around in the room, he knew he had to own up to some things.

"I never got the chance to apologize for accusing you of being your own secret admirer."

"Mr. Winters interrupted us at a bad time."

Matt would have let it go at that, because that was the truth. But he felt guilty that she had so easily made an excuse for him and forgiven him when he didn't always do the same for her.

"Yeah, but I should have realized you wouldn't send yourself candy. It was a dumb conclusion to jump to."

"I made my own share of dumb conclusions on this,

Matt. Don't forget I assumed you sent both arrangements of roses."

Matt's thoughts automatically drifted back to the day she'd told him that. It was the day he had gone to her apartment to apologize for kissing her. In his mind's eye, he could see her in the short pink chenille robe, see the long length of her leg exposed. He also remembered that was the day she told him she had a crush on him.

A thousand feelings bombarded him, including his undeniable attraction to her and the fact that they were so different from each other. She might be kind and generous, but Matt didn't think he could live with someone so ruthlessly spontaneous and so willing to cast her future to the Fates.

He also knew why. And he also knew that having come this far with him Sarah deserved to know, too.

"I told you that my mother left my father when I was about ten, right?"

Sarah said, "Uh-huh."

"Well, she didn't keep in touch with us after she left."

"Are you trying to explain why you're gun-shy about commitment?"

"No, I'm trying to explain why we ended up with such opposite personalities. I'd like to be as open and fun as you are, but the things that happened in my life led me to be more cautious."

He felt her roll to face him. "So, why didn't your mother keep in touch?"

"Because of what my dad called bad memories. He didn't explain much about the breakup of their marriage, except that he took responsibility for the fact that money was always tight and my mother was always doing without. He said at a certain point she snapped.''

''Snapped?''

''She didn't go insane or anything like that, but she just couldn't take it anymore.''

''And you never saw her again?'' Sarah asked incredulously. She pushed herself off the pillow and half sat up, facing him in the darkness. It blew her away to think that a woman could desert her child, but didn't surprise her that Matt had rationalized it.

''No. Think it through, Sarah, I was part of the bad memories.''

''I guess.''

In the thin light coming into the room from parking-lot lights, Sarah saw Matt hazard a glance in her direction. ''We've already talked about the fact that you've never been poor…''

Sarah grimaced. ''Right.''

''And that keeps you from understanding things that I've lived.'' He peeked at her again. ''When you're always scraping to get by, there comes a point where people break, Sarah. My mother reached hers.''

Sarah couldn't argue that. She didn't know what it was like to hate being poor the way his mother had any more than she could understand what it was like to be deserted. Matt must have felt terribly unwanted to have built this wall around himself to prevent that kind of pain again. But she did know that he had built a wall. And that explained a lot of things. Like why he hadn't noticed her until she'd forced him to look. And why he kept pulling back.

''Do you realize what you're telling me?''

''I'm telling you that my mother was human, and I'm

not going to hold it against her that she reached the end of her rope and made a new life for herself."

Sarah said simply, "You're a better person than I am."

Matt laughed. "No, you're a better person than I am, Sarah. You're spontaneous and funny and bold enough to go after everything you want."

Sarah winced, realizing that if she really was bold enough to go after what she wanted she'd be naked in his arms right now. "Growing up on a ranch will do that for you."

Matt laughed again. "I suppose." He paused a second, then asked, "So what is it like to grow up on a ranch?"

"It's different, way different than living in a city like Boston. You make do with what you have in a lot of ways, because there isn't a mall in every town or a fast-food restaurant on every corner. But, on the bright side, because you have to rely on your wits a lot more, people don't judge as much by looks. They react to substance."

"That makes sense."

Sarah yawned. "Yeah. It does."

"You didn't have trouble adjusting."

Sarah laughed, then yawned again. "What do you think the last year was all about?"

"Adjusting?"

"Yeah. It took me that long to brave getting a makeover and really become a part of things."

"Right."

"So, are we done talking?" Sarah asked, yawning again.

"Yeah," Matt said, but he didn't mean it. He could have talked to her all night. He'd never realized how good it would feel to tell somebody about his mother and not have her react with pity. And he supposed that was another point in Sarah's favor. In her own way, she was as pragmatic as he was.

Still, he didn't say anything else. Instead, he stayed quiet with his thoughts, waiting for the sound of the deep, even breathing that signaled that she was asleep.

The last thing he remembered was closing his eyes and beginning to count backward from a thousand so he would get enough rest to drive them back to Boston in the morning. And his next conscious thought was that something was tickling his nose.

He shook his head to try to rid himself of the offending tickle, and discovered his nose was buried in someone's hair. Sarah's hair. He smiled and inhaled deeply. But then he realized they were spooned together like lovers, huddled into each other's warmth in a position that spoke of affection and intimacy, and he immediately scooted away.

Sarah, however, followed him.

Great. Now what? If he moved over any farther, he'd end up on the floor. He had to get out of bed.

He inhaled deeply, breathing in the scent of her hair again, knowing he wasn't going anywhere. Even though it was daylight and time to get up, he didn't want to leave—at least not for another minute. Physically, he'd never been more attracted to a woman. Mentally, he'd never been more distant from one. He wished he could chuck common sense and make love to her, and force himself to fall headfirst into an ill-fated relationship with her, but he knew he couldn't. The very fact that he couldn't think of a relationship with her without using the word *ill-fated,* proved he knew it was doomed, and he couldn't set himself or Sarah up for failure. He didn't want to see either one of them hurt.

With that thought, he shifted slightly to get himself away from temptation, but Sarah's arm tightened around him. He moved to slide her arm away, but as he did he saw her eyes were open and everything inside him froze.

"Good morning."

He cleared his throat. "Good morning."

"I guess nature sort of took its own course last night," she said as she rolled from their spoon position to face him.

"Which is exactly why I need to get out of bed right now."

Her green eyes searched his for a second before she said, "Why don't you kiss me instead?"

He groaned. "Don't do this."

She smiled. "Why not? I swear what we do this morning won't go beyond this room."

He gaped at her. "You would have casual sex with me?"

She held his gaze again. "If I had sex with you, there would be nothing casual about it."

Matt groaned again, but Sarah only smiled. "You can't leave, can you?"

"But I'm not supposed to stay, either."

Sarah laughed and slid her arms around his neck. "Your body is singing a very different tune," she said, before she pulled his head to hers and kissed him deeply.

Matt felt himself spiraling out of control. She was so warm, so soft and so perfect that he wanted nothing more than the chance to make love to her. He slid his hand up and down her bare arm, feeling the baggy T-shirt he had lent to her, knowing he could probably get it over her head with one quick yank. Then he

wouldn't be feeling cotton against his palm, he would
be feeling the smooth velvet of her skin, the crisp lace
of her bra.

His chest tightened, along with everything else in his
body. He wanted her so badly, he thought he'd die from
it.

But he also refused to hurt her.

Still, he couldn't quite pull himself away from their
long, lingering kiss because he felt he deserved at least
that for the gallantry he was about to display. Knowing
he would never get a chance to be with her this way
again, he let himself enjoy her warm, wet mouth. With
his hands cupping her head, he savored the sensation of
his tongue twining with hers, the satiny smoothness of
her lips, even the softness of her hair beneath his fingers.

Reaction after reaction ricocheted through him. He
wanted to touch every inch of her skin, wanted to kiss
her forever. His body responded with a longing so intense, Matt slid his hands down her hair to her arms
and across the T-shirt he had lent her. She inched closer,
her hands leaving the security of his neck and drifting
to caress his chest. Of their own volition, it seemed,
Matt's hands followed suit, skipping across her soft cotton covering until one of them found the hardened nip-
ple of one of her breasts. His fingers caressed the delicate peak. Their kiss deepened. The sights and sounds
of their hotel room drifted away and all of life funneled
down to what he was doing, what he could feel and
how Sarah made him feel.

Steeped with need, he reached for the hem of the
T-shirt, slid his hand beneath and was welcomed by
soft, warm flesh. His eager fingers danced up her torso,

caressing her ribs and unerringly found the breast he had been touching through her shirt.

Without warning, desire shot through Matt. He was overwhelmed with the kind of primal urge he suspected inspired men to do things like renounce their kingdoms, leave their quiet lives and walk away from long-held goals. In that second, nothing in the world mattered to him except stripping her naked and showing her the kind of impact she had on him. The need consumed him. It solidified his muscles, brought his blood to a near boil and almost—almost—completely muddled his thoughts. But not quite.

Because he knew making love to her wasn't right. The only thing it would accomplish would be to show them what they couldn't have. When they were done making love, they still wouldn't be able to commit the way lovers were supposed to commit. But more than that, after making love to her, resisting temptation would be harder because they both would know what they were missing.

Realizing that if he didn't pull away now they'd both be in trouble, he broke the kiss, shifting his mouth away from hers, and stared into her soft green eyes for a second. Then he said, "I would love to do this. In fact, there are parts of me that are sure I will die if I don't do this. But I can't I can't hurt you. I don't want to get hurt myself and one of us would surely get hurt if we made love."

Chapter Nine

That night Sarah showed up at Carmella's door. "Come in! Come in!" Carmella said, pulling Sarah inside. "I was so worried! My goodness, getting stuck in a hurricane and then having to spend the night in a hotel! I can see why Lloyd told you to take today off. Are you okay?"

"I'm great," Sarah said cautiously, allowing Carmella to lead her into her living room.

"Can I get you some coffee or tea or something?"

"No. I just want to talk."

"Okay," Carmella said, taking the seat beside Sarah on the nubby tweed sofa of the comfortable room. Hardwood floors picked up the light of the fire in the gas fireplace. Green plants decorated the end tables, hung from the ceiling and sat in a corner plant stand. The room was warm and alive, very much like Carmella herself. "I can tell something happened. What was it?"

"Well, there was only one room available at the hotel," Sarah began, knowing she didn't have to explain that she had come here to talk about Matt. Her suspicions were confirmed when Carmella gasped.

"You slept together!"

"*Slept* being the correct word," Sarah said with a sigh. "I couldn't seduce a man who didn't want to be seduced."

Carmella's eyes widened. "You almost seduced him?"

"Yes." Sarah combed her fingers through her hair, so confused by Matt she didn't know where to start. "Carmella, did you know his mother left his dad?"

She nodded. "Yes."

"Do you know why?"

"Something about money…"

"Yes. But as women we know her reasons for leaving had to be greater than that. A woman doesn't desert a child for money. Even if she fell in love with another man, she wouldn't give up her son. There's something wrong in that story."

"What does this have to do with you and Matt?"

That was a very good question. What did that have to do with her and Matt? Sarah wasn't exactly sure, but she did know all the pieces of Matt's story didn't fit. And she needed Carmella to hear as many of them as she had heard to see if, as an objective listener, Carmella drew the same conclusions as she had.

She took a quick breath and said, "According to Matt, his mother *chose* never to see him again. And I can't help but think that makes him afraid of commitment, and that's the real reason he can't seem to have a relationship with me."

Carmella pondered that. "Truthfully, Sarah, he told me that he doesn't want to have a relationship with anybody until he's financially stable."

"He doesn't think he's financially stable now?"

"No. He wants to be a multimillionaire before he's forty."

Sarah shook her head. "I'm not surprised. In fact, that actually fits with the conclusions I'm drawing about his mother. According to Matt, his mother left because she and his father were always scraping by." She paused and sighed. "But that's still not a reason to leave your child and *never* see him again. I can't help but feel money is just the tip of the iceberg in this story."

Carmella shrugged. "Probably. Emotions always run deeper than bank accounts."

"Which means there's something we don't know. Think about it. Even if all the bare facts are correct. Even if Matt's mother did *choose* never to see her son again, one little detail could make the story totally different. Especially if there was a very good reason she decided to stay away. And if the story was totally different, if there was a 'reason' Matt's mother chose to stay away from him, Matt's whole perception of relationships and commitment could change. Just like that," Sarah said, snapping her fingers.

Carmella silently considered that, then asked, "So, how do we fix this?"

Sarah took a long breath. "I think we're going to have to find his mother and talk to her."

"Do you really think that's a good idea?"

"I think it's the only idea." Sarah shrugged. "Matt keeps order in his life like someone who's trying to make sure nothing goes wrong. And if you think that through, it could mean he can't enter into a relationship because he knows no one can control everything about a relationship. He can admit he has feelings for me, but can't do anything about them. He says we're opposites, but I think I scare him.''

Carmella laughed. "Honey, with your new look you scared a lot of the men.''

Not in the mood for humor, Sarah shook her head. "That's not what I'm saying.''

"I know.'' Carmella patted Sarah's hand. "What you're saying is perfectly logical. You're saying that you think that if his mother had a good reason for not wanting to see him, Matt would realize life isn't so capricious.''

"Exactly. Then he might be willing to step out and do something without having fifty safety nets.''

Carmella sighed. "Okay, you're probably right.'' She sighed again. "So what do you want to do?''

"We'll never convince Matt to go looking for his mother. But if my guess is correct about the end of his parents' marriage, I'm pretty sure that his mother will be eager to find him. If she left Matt's dad for a good reason, Matt's dad might not have been too thrilled to admit that or talk about the situation, but his mother might, if only to get back into her son's life. So, no matter what it takes, we need to find her.''

Carmella rose from her seat. "Come on, let's go look on the Internet for Matt's mom.''

That night Matt sat at his desk in his apartment, reading the same paragraph of a Wintersoft contract over and over and over again, because he couldn't concentrate. His thoughts kept tiptoeing back to Sarah and what it felt like to be lying in her arms.

He wasn't preoccupied with the sexual end of things, though he would be lying to himself if he pretended the sexual part of their relationship didn't try to sneak in.

The truth was, the thing he remembered most about sleeping with Sarah was the feeling of comfort. Rightness. Security.

He'd never felt that with another woman…hell, he'd never felt it with another person, except his dad, and he had the sense that if he didn't pursue these feelings he had for her he would be very, very sorry.

He liked her. And the other emotion that kept sneaking up on him when he least expected it was that he was happy. He'd been happy before, of course. He'd even been happy with women, but never happy because of a woman. He began to suspect that Sarah was right. He probably did have trust issues. And the impulsive, spontaneous, slightly out-of-the-ordinary woman that Sarah was, she might just be the person who could help him get over them.

He shook his head. He didn't know, because everything kept getting confused. His logical mind couldn't wrap around the possibility that loving Sarah could make everything better, even if his heart did believe it was true. But he did know he had to do something about Sarah soon, or he wasn't ever going to get any work done!

Matt didn't speak much to Sarah the following day at work, so she was completely surprised when he showed up at her apartment Friday night.

"Matt! What are you doing here?"

He shrugged and stuffed his hands in the front pockets of his jeans. "You know, I'm not really sure myself."

"Want to come in?"

"Yeah," he said, smiling as he followed the motion of her hand and entered her apartment. He looked so different in jeans and a sweatshirt, so comfortable, so relaxed—so cute—that Sarah could only stare at him.

"Can I get you some coffee or something?"

He shook his head. "It'll keep me awake later."

Thinking about his typical overly alert nature, Sarah smiled. "Yeah, I guess it would."

"Can we sit?"

"Sure," Sarah said and took the seat on the chair since he sat on the sofa.

But he patted the cushion beside him. "I think for this discussion you should sit beside me."

Sarah's heart jumped to triple time. Being near him always caused a riot in her nervous system, but tonight, with the unexpected visit and his unexpected look, the situation was even more fraught with tension. He obviously had something he wanted to tell her, and he wanted her *beside* him when he said it.

Every cell in Sarah's body tingled with expectancy, but remembering this was pragmatic Matt, she stifled any hope that his announcement might be something romantic. She calmly rose and sat demurely beside him on the sofa, but when he took her hand she couldn't stop the sweet anticipation that threaded through her.

"I've been thinking a lot about us."

The sense of anticipation grew, tightening her chest. "Really?"

He caught her gaze. "You haven't?"

"Of course I have," she said, sighing heavily because practical Matt would never let her get away with being cute, coy or coquettish. "Some days I do nothing but think about us! There! Are you happy?"

Surprisingly, he laughed. "Yes, actually. That's why I was so quiet today. Last night, I realized that for the first time in a long while I felt happy."

That completely astounded her. Happy people were normally bubbly. But, then again, Matt always broke the mold and did things his own way. "Really? You were quiet because you were happy?"

"Yes. I was happy, but I was also quiet because I was thinking things through."

She looked at their linked hands. "Apparently, you've come to some conclusions."

He caught her gaze again. "A couple. First, I really, really like you. We might be opposites, but I like that you're enthusiastic. Sometimes even your unpredictability is fun."

Sarah would have thanked him but she was too busy holding her breath.

"Second, I respect your differences and I would be willing to work around them, if you would be willing to respect mine and not expect me to change."

"Oh, Matt! I would never want you to change! I like you the way you are!"

He smiled at her. "And I like you, too. But I still haven't told you my third conclusion."

This time it was fear that threaded through her. Only the Lord knew what his third conclusion could be. "Okay."

"Actually, there are two more things. First, if we were to get romantically involved, I think we would need to keep it out of the office, at least until we know if we really could be serious about each other."

Too shocked for words, Sarah nodded her agreement.

"Second, we would have to take this slowly. I want to sleep with you more than I want my next breath of air, but I've also seen things go sour very quickly. And for no apparent reason. So, I want to be sure."

"I agree," Sarah said, though inside she was floating.

He liked her enough that he was willing to accept her as she was and she almost couldn't believe it. They would go slowly, but at least they would be working toward everything she wanted, and at this point she couldn't ask for anything more than that.

Particularly since she hadn't yet found his mother. The bottom line to all Matt's trust issues was his mother's desertion. If Sarah could find her and convince her to come back into Matt's life—especially with an explanation of why she had left and never seen him— she knew she could help him heal his wounds.

"So what are we allowed to do?"

He caught her gaze and solemnly said, "I was hoping we could have a date or two before we made any real decisions."

"Sounds fair."

"And I was also thinking I should be allowed to kiss you."

Sarah smiled. "Sounds wonderful."

And it was. When he touched his mouth to hers, Sarah felt as if she were in heaven. He was warm and wonderful and so very, very real that she savored the lips caressing hers, and reveled in the strength of the corded muscles beneath her trembling hands. He might not love her. He might not *ever* love her, but he was at least going to give her a chance.

And she was making the most of it, not just by working with him to overcome their differences but also by finding his mother so he could see there was nothing wrong with him and no reason to be distrustful anymore. Especially of her.

Saturday afternoon, Sarah walked with Carmella up the sidewalk of the elaborate ranch house owned by

Mary Jane Oswald, Matt's mother. Though the house itself was ornate and elegant, the neighborhood was modest. The car in the driveway was more than a few years old.

"I thought Matt said his mother left his dad for money?"

"He did," Sarah said, pressing the doorbell. "But the very fact that we didn't find her in a castle proves my theory that there's more to this divorce than meets the eye."

Carmella glanced around. "Well, technically, this is a castle of sorts. The house itself is bigger and better kept than the ones around it. Maybe Matt's mother and her husband enjoy being the big fish in the small pond?"

The door opened and a tall, slender woman said, "Hi. Can I help you?"

"Mrs. Oswald?"

The woman nodded. "Yes."

"I'm Sarah Morris and this is Carmella Lopez. We work with your son, Matt."

"Yes. Hi," Mary Jane Oswald said, smiling from Sarah to Carmella. "I spoke with Carmella on the phone."

"It's nice to meet you in person," Carmella said, leaning forward to shake Mary Jane's hand.

"Come in."

Sarah and Carmella stepped into the small, overly decorated foyer of the house. Sarah noticed again that though the structure itself appeared to be nothing more than a typical ranch house, the decorations and furniture were expensive.

"We'll talk in the den," Mary Jane said and led Car-mella and Sarah down the hall. She turned on the overhead light and revealed a well-tended room with hard-wood floors, an Oriental accent rug and leather furniture.

"Wow," Carmella said as she sat on one of the two chairs in front of the desk. "This room is gorgeous."

"Thank you." Mary Jane took the seat behind the desk. "Since my husband's passing I've been shifting everything from his taste to mine. This time last year this poor room had tacky wall-to-wall carpet and a collection of antique spittoons."

Sarah laughed, but Carmella glanced around thoughtfully. "I didn't expect to find a room this big in this part of the house."

"Because we didn't have kids," Mary Jane said, getting comfortable on the tall-backed black leather chair, "we consolidated two bedrooms."

"Well, it is lovely," Carmella said, smiling at Mary Jane.

"Yes, it's lovely," Sarah echoed. Nerves danced along her skin. Though Carmella's questions and comments sounded innocent, Sarah knew exactly where she had been going with them. Not only had she painlessly discovered that Matt's mother's husband was dead, she'd also learned Matt had no half brothers and sisters.

And all that added up to the fact that Mary Jane Oswald could be as much in need of a reconciliation with her son as Matt was in need of a relationship with his mother.

"So, you told me on the phone that you work with my son," Mary Jane said to Carmella.

"I'm executive assistant for the owner of the company Matt works for and Sarah is Matt's assistant."

Mary Jane leaned forward. "Oh, so he has his own assistant."

"He heads an entire department," Sarah said, but Carmella gave her a light kick, reminding her that they had decided in the car that they didn't want to give away too much information about Matt. If or when he met his mother, what to reveal and what to withhold should be his choice.

Mary Jane's eyes brightened. "He does?"

"Yes. He's a CPA," Sarah said. "And he works very hard, but we didn't exactly come here to talk about Matt. We'd like to hear about you."

Mary Jane shook her head. "That means he's a failure."

Sarah gasped. "He's not a failure."

"Well, not exactly a failure," Mary Jane said with a shrug. "More like middle management. Just like his father."

Carmella said, "You say that as if being like his dad is bad."

"It's not bad. It's just typical. Average. Matt's father worked his fool head off and never got anywhere."

Sarah looked around. She'd met Matt's dad, and had even been to his house for a party once. As far as she could tell by comparing the size and location of Mary Jane's house to the size and location of Matt's dad's house, Wayne Burke had been as successful as Mary Jane's husband had been. Of course, for all Sarah knew, Mary Jane could have tons of money in the bank.

Continuing the questioning that Carmella had started, Sarah asked, "And that's what broke up your marriage?"

Mary Jane fiddled with a pen on her desk, as if debating answering the personal question. "You make me sound short-tempered and greedy, but I wasn't. Wayne had tons of ambition and more potential than anybody else I knew. But when he passed the exam to become a CPA, he sort of stopped. The whole time he went to school he also worked a full-time job, so he knew how to put in a fourteen-hour day. I felt that when he got his degree and a job in his field, he would work lots of overtime and fight his way up the corporate ladder. Instead, he came home every day at five. Our lives settled in and I started to feel like a rat in a trap.''

This part of the story meshed with what Matt had told her, so Sarah said, ''And that's why you left.''

''Precisely. My late husband, Mark, became a partner in the accounting firm for which he worked and by the time he was fifty-five he could retire. We had an active social life.'' She drew a long breath, obviously remembering. ''I miss it.''

Sarah thought that through and said, ''That makes perfect sense. I left North Dakota because I felt out of place there too.''

''Really?''

Sarah smiled. ''Yes. I lived on a ranch with my parents and literally got so bored I knew I had to get out.''

''Precisely,'' Mary Jane said, beaming with the pleasure of being understood.

The connection between them firmly established, Sarah recognized there would be no better time to ask the question that had actually brought her and Carmella to Matt's mother's home. ''I'm just a little bit confused about why you never contacted Matt.''

''Excuse me?''

''Why didn't you ever visit Matt?''

Mary Jane's eyes darkened with anger and Sarah knew that no matter how good their connection the question had not been welcome. ''I don't see what business that is of yours…''

"Finding out about you is the entire purpose for our visit," Carmella said, jumping in to save Sarah. "I told you that when I called. I told you to expect some questions."

"Because I thought Matt was sick or something... Is he?"

"No. He's perfectly healthy."

"So I don't need to go and stand by his bed and make my peace with him before he dies?"

Sarah laughed. "Heavens, no!"

"Then what is the purpose for this visit?"

"Matt is unhappy and we think part of his unhappiness might stem from..."

"From me not being involved in his life," Mary Jane speculated defensively. Then she shook her head with disgust. "You people kill me. Look at you. All dressed up, zipping around, trying to make the world a better place for my son." She glanced from Sarah to Carmella then back to Sarah again. "Do you think I'm stupid? You," she said, pointing at Sarah, "probably have a crush on him and he's rebuffed you. So you're thinking that if you can bring him back together with his estranged mother you'll win brownie points or something and he'll fall at your feet."

She rose from her seat and rounded the desk. "Undoubtedly, he has money of some sort. Otherwise you wouldn't be interested. And since that's the case, I'm sure he isn't so witless that he'd fall for such a cheap ploy, and I certainly don't want any part of it." She strode to the den door, dismissing Sarah and Carmella. "Good day."

Carmella rose without a second's hesitation. Sarah felt so odd she almost couldn't stand. The woman who openly admitted she had left Wayne Burke for a man with more money had just—in a roundabout way—called her a gold digger.

Though Carmella was halfway to the door, she stopped and faced Sarah again. "Sarah? Come on."

"Okay," Sarah said, lifting herself from the chair. When she reached the door, she paused, looked at Matt's mother and tried to say something but nothing would come out. Part of her wanted to defend herself. The other part was too astonished to try.

"Good day, Mrs. Oswald," she said, then turned and walked up the hall. She followed Carmella out into the bright sunshine and silently got into her car.

"Well, she's certainly a nutcase," Carmella said as Sarah backed her car out of the driveway.

"Nutcase doesn't even hit the tip of the iceberg. Do you believe she accused me of chasing Matt for his money, when she all but came right out and admitted that was why she married Mark Oswald and abandoned her only child?"

"Don't be too offended. People don't usually see their own sins. Plus, she obviously doesn't know money is the last thing you would chase anyone for since your family isn't even close to being poor." Carmella laughed unexpectedly. "And that might be a good thing since I'm just about certain that if she did know your family had money, she would have turned herself into your best friend."

"No kidding!" Sarah said, making the turns necessary to get back on the highway. "She's definitely a dead end."

"So, what are you going to do about Matt?"

"I don't know."

"Well, one thing's for certain," Carmella said, "We don't want to connect Matt and his mother. It would only reinforce his belief that money talks. Or worse that people can't be trusted.''

"Agreed!"

Obviously considering the situation, Carmella gnawed her lower lip. "Maybe we shouldn't even mention to him that we met her.''

Sarah sighed with relief. "My thought exactly.''

Matt showed up at Sarah's apartment again on Saturday night. He held two bags of Chinese food.

"See, when I want to be, I can be spontaneous, too.''

Thrilled to see him, Sarah grinned. "Yes, you can.'' But her joy was immediately overshadowed by the memory of meeting his mother. She didn't like keeping a secret from him, but though half of her thought she should tell him, the other half knew telling him she had found and visited his mother would only dredge up bad memories for him. Maybe even make matters worse. Matt had clearly rationalized his mother's behavior and didn't need to hear any more details or stories. Sarah wished she had left well enough alone, but since she hadn't, she could take comfort in checking Matt's mother off the list of ways to get Matt to trust again. If nothing else, knowing Matt's mother was a dead end pointed her in a better direction.

He strode into her living room and deposited the bags on her coffee table. Then he turned and caught her by the elbows and pulled her close. "I called and left a message on your machine that I was coming over, but apparently you didn't get it.''

His nearness was enough to make her swoon. "I was preoccupied when I got home this afternoon and forgot to check my messages.''

"Where were you?" he asked, smiling and Sarah's heart tripped into double time.

The speed-up wasn't only the result of being so close to good-looking, warm, strong and wonderful Matt. His continued questions pressed down on the weight of keeping her meeting with his mother from him. But though the weight was heavy, Sarah also knew it was far better to keep the secret than tell him the horrible truth about his mother.

She rose to her tiptoes and brushed her lips across his, realizing that she now understood how he felt about her secret admirer. Though Matt didn't have any evidence that the guy sending her flowers and candy was a stalker, he worried for her safety. Sarah had seen for herself that his mother was a strange woman and a strong protective instinct rose up in her too. Not only would she keep him from Mary Jane Oswald, but also she intended to make up for every miserable impression he had about women because of the woman.

"Thank you for supper."

Matt smiled, then returned her kiss. "You're welcome." He paused, then smiled again. "You know, I like this."

"Relationships can be fun."

He shook his head. "I've had lots of relationships, but never with someone I felt so close to." He caught her gaze. "We don't know every little detail of each other's lives but we've been together forty hours a week for an entire year. All this feels very natural."

"It does for me, too," Sarah agreed.

"I'm glad you pushed me."

"I'm glad I pushed you, too."

He frowned and tried to look threatening. "Let's just not make a habit of it."

She skipped away. "Now that I have what I want, you'll find I'm perfectly mannerly."

"You haven't exactly gotten what you want."

"So we're saving the good stuff for later," Sarah said, grabbing one of the cartons of food and plopping to the sofa. "I can deal with that."

"I can, too."

Sarah nearly breathed a sigh of relief, but she didn't. No matter how good the situation with Matt looked, she knew it was still up in the air.

And she also knew that at some point, she was going to have to admit she had met his mother. She couldn't keep the secret forever. It wouldn't be fair.

The next few days passed in a blur of bliss for Sarah. Matt had a long-standing every-other-night dinner date with his dad, so they couldn't spend every spare minute in each other's company, but Sarah thought that was probably good. However, she was a tad miffed that he hadn't asked her to attend Lloyd Winters's annual charity ball with him.

Still, not wanting to look for trouble, Sarah rationalized the situation. As a member of the support staff, she got a free ticket from Lloyd. As a senior vice president, Matt was expected to purchase his own and make a hefty donation. They both had to attend, and Sarah realized Matt might believe that asking her to go would be redundant.

Plus, their going to a Wintersoft event together was the ultimate test of their relationship. It would be the first time they were seen together in public. She wasn't surprised when Matt was silent the day before the event, apparently worried about how they should behave at a dinner dance being attended by everyone they worked with.

Sarah also wasn't surprised when he stopped by her desk at quitting time and very quietly said, "You and I need to talk."

She peeked up from her work and smiled. "Really."

"Yes," Matt said. He glanced at Grant's door and noticed it was closed, then waited until Sunny gathered her things to leave for the day before he said, "Would you please come into my office?"

Confused, Sarah looked at him. Though they had agreed to keep their personal relationship out of the workplace, Matt hadn't been this stiff and formal in days. His reverting back to his old behavior scared her into thinking he might want to ask her to stay away from him at the ball.

"Now?" Sarah said just as Sunny walked past her desk.

"See you in the morning, Sarah. Matt."

"Yeah, see you tomorrow, Sunny," Matt said cheerfully and Sarah rose from her chair. His agreeable tone of voice made Sarah believe she must have imagined the tension she'd thought she'd heard when he first stopped at her desk.

Matt indicated that she should precede him into the room and she walked in and took the seat in front of his desk. "What do you want to talk about?"

"Why don't you try taking a wild guess?"

Sarah laughed. From his cool, terse tone she realized the strain of being seen together in public when their relationship was so fragile was too much for Matt's pragmatic mind to deal with and she decided to relent. If she let him off the hook for this event, there would be other charity balls. She could be patient.

"Look. If this is about us being together at the charity ball, I'll understand if you're not ready to be seen in public with me yet."

"This has nothing to do with the ball," Matt said, taking his seat behind the desk. "Yesterday afternoon, I realized that we would have to make a public appearance sometime and the charity ball was as good of a chance as any. I had intended to ask you to go with me this morning."

"You had," she said, confused. "But you didn't."

"No. I didn't. Because my mother visited me last night."

Sarah gasped as fear filled her. "Oh, no! Oh, Matt I'm so sorry!"

"And she told me two people I work with approached her because one of them has a crush on me."

"I never said…" Sarah began, but Matt clearly didn't want to hear it.

"What the hell were you thinking!"

"Not at all what you're assuming!" Sarah said desperately. "Matt, I almost told you on Saturday night…"

"I wish you had."

"I couldn't. Everything between us is so new. And what I did was wrong. But I didn't know that until after I went to see her. I thought if I could bring her into your life I could make things better. But she's not the kind of mother I expected to find."

Matt tapped his pencil on his desk blotter. "She hit me up for fifty thousand dollars."

Sarah clutched her chest. "Oh, my God!"

"She made the request as if I somehow owe her."

Sarah stifled a horrified gasp. "I'm so sorry."

"She seemed to believe that since she gave me life. I should give her money."

"Matt, *I am so sorry.*"

"You haven't even heard the good part yet, Sarah. She warned me there was a gold-digger female in my office, trying to sink her claws into me and for a mere ten thousand dollars a visit, she'd come into the office and put you in your place...the way she handled you on Saturday."

Sarah only stared at Matt.

"The woman is ruthless, Sarah. That's why I stayed away from her. That's why my dad was thrilled to see her marry right after she left. I once overheard him tell one of his friends that as soon as she remarried she'd become somebody else's problem."

"But you seemed to need closure."

"I got closure when I was fifteen, when she divorced her second husband and married her third. I saw that she had decided the best way to increase her standard of living was to go from husband to husband."

Sarah frowned. "So, if you saw through her when you were fifteen, why are you playing into her theories?"

"I'm not playing into her theories!"

"You told Carmella you can't marry until you're a multimillionaire, which means you believe she was right. You think women marry for money."

"Is that what you think?"

"That's what you *say!*"

"I say that because I do intend to keep my financial goals. But I've also said all along, Sarah, that we're different. Opposites. And this just proves it. There's no way in hell I'd have the guts to interfere in another person's life the way you've interfered in mine."

Righteous indignation rose to save Sarah. "Oh, really. Who is it that called my secret admirer a stalker?

Who is it that insisted on accompanying me to the florist? Who is it that made his own trip to the gift shop to discover the identity of the candy sender?''

''That was different.''

''How?''

''When it comes to your secret admirer, you don't know who you're dealing with. When it comes to my mother, I know exactly who she is.''

''So you were trying to protect me.''

''Yes.''

''By interfering.''

''No!''

''Then what do you call it?''

Matt sighed heavily. ''Okay, we can go on like this forever because we obviously see the situation two different ways. So let's stop now.''

Sarah nodded her agreement.

Matt raised his eyes until he caught her gaze and said, ''But that only proves my point. The real point I've been trying to make all along. We're too different, Sarah. Much too different to consider being in a relationship.''

''But…''

''We'd drive each other crazy in six months.'' He held her gaze. ''Do you want that? Do you want to end up hating each other?''

Biting her bottom lip, Sarah shook her head.

''Neither do I.''

He rose from his seat, signaling the end of the conversation. ''I also think you need to request a transfer. If I ask for you to be placed in another department it will raise all kinds of questions. If you go on your own, everybody will just think you're looking for something different.''

Sarah nodded.

"Good. Put in your request for a transfer first thing tomorrow.''

Chapter Ten

Friday morning, Sarah walked into the office of the Senior Vice President of Human Resources, Melinda McIntosh, and set her neatly typed request for departmental transfer on her desk.

"Sarah?" Melinda said, looking up from her work. Tall and blond, with big blue eyes and a wide smile, the forty-something VP was the picture of the perfect female executive in her navy-blue suit and white silk blouse. "This is a surprise," she said glancing at the request for transfer. "I thought you loved the accounting department."

Sarah shrugged. "I'm a little bored."

Melinda leaned back in her chair. "Really?"

"Yeah."

"Let's see, in the past month you've acquired a secret admirer and totally changed your look. Now, you want to switch jobs." She paused a second as she thought that through. "Are you sure you might not be making one change too many?"

Sarah smiled as brightly as she could to hide the fact that Melinda was right. She *had* made too many changes. Everything in her life had spun out of control. The last thing she wanted to do was step into a new department and learn a new job. But she also didn't want to work with a man she'd lost because she'd made a mistake and he was now one step away from hating her. The tension between them would be unbearable.

"I'm sure."

"Okay," Melinda said, smiling as she scooped up Sarah's request for transfer and slid it into the bottom slot of her in-basket. "I'll spread the word and see if anybody's interested in getting a very competent assistant." She frowned. "Hmm. This also means I have to find somebody else for Matt. Does he know you put in a request for transfer?"

Sarah decided not to duck the truth. Without going into detail of why, she said, "He suggested it."

"Well, my day is just full of surprises!" Melinda shook her head then smiled at Sarah again. "I'll call you as soon as I have a nibble."

"Okay," Sarah said and left Melinda's office. With her head down and her thoughts in turmoil, she almost bumped into Nelson. He steadied her by catching her shoulders.

"Whoa! Where are you going in such a hurry?"

"Back to my office."

He looked around as if confused. "What were you doing down here in personnel?"

Deciding the whole office would find out soon enough anyway, Sarah shrugged and said, "Requesting a transfer."

"Out of *Matt's* department?" Nelson asked incredulously.

She nodded. "Yeah."

"Wow. Does this mean you're on the market again?"

Sarah frowned at the way he phrased that. "What?"

"Does this mean you're on the market?" he repeated. When she only stared at him, he added, "Willing to go into any department?"

"Oh. Yeah. I'm ready to go to the highest bidder," she said, laughing slightly, trying to lighten the mood.

But Nelson didn't laugh. "I just can't believe you're suddenly transferring out of accounting."

"This has been coming for a long time."

"Really? I never noticed it."

Since she had to come up with a good excuse that everyone would accept, Sarah decided to try out the most obvious explanation on Nelson. "Yeah. You remember I got flowers from a secret admirer?"

"Twice. You also got candy."

"Well, I also got lots of visitors. Matt didn't approve and we started arguing. Our work suffered. We're not a good team anymore."

"So you could say your secret admirer split you two up?"

Again, his phrasing sounded off, as if he thought of her and Matt more as a couple than boss and assistant, but because Nelson was one of the computer nerds, not someone wholly versed in male/female relationships, she dismissed it.

"Yeah. I guess you could say that." She glanced at her watch. "And I also have to get going."

"Me, too. I got a notice from human resources that Mr. Winters wants to see me and Melinda this afternoon, but I don't have time. So I'm going to try and see if I can change the meeting to Monday."

Sarah laughed. "You're trying to change a meeting with Mr. Winters?"

Nelson looked at her as if she were crazy. "Getting ready for year-end is my busy time of year. I don't have time to meet with him."

"Most people make time, Nelson!"

Nelson shook his head. "This is why you and Matt stopped getting along. He would understand why I can't meet with Lloyd."

Since it was obvious she didn't understand Matt, Sarah couldn't argue.

Nelson said goodbye to Sarah and she headed for her office.

She couldn't decide if she dreaded spending the day with Matt because she knew he was angry with her, or because she knew it would be one of their last days together. There would be no more second chances for them. Not because he was stubborn or adamant, but because he was right. Her interference in his personal life did prove that she was bold. And he wasn't. He was thoughtful, deliberate about everything. No matter how much she loved him, she drove him crazy. And that made the pain even worse. She was not a loveable person to the man she absolutely adored.

At her workstation, she opened the bottom drawer of her desk and shoved her purse inside at the same time that Matt arrived for the day.

"Good morning, Sarah," he said. With his nose in the newspaper, he reminded her of Grant. But also with his nose in the newspaper Sarah knew he wouldn't see the sadness in her eyes when she looked at him.

Gazing at his solid body she remembered waking up in his arms in New Hampshire. She remembered the warmth of him. The sweet, masculine scent. The feeling of protection and love she had felt with his arms wrapped around her. She wanted to weep. It didn't seem fair that two people who were so physically attracted to each other could be so wrong for each other. But they were.

"Did you do the errand I requested last night?"

She cleared her throat. "You said first thing. So I made it my first thing. Melinda has my paperwork."

"Paperwork for what?" Carmella asked, walking toward Sarah's workstation.

Matt glanced at Sunny's desk, Sarah knew, to be sure she hadn't yet arrived, before he said, "I asked Sarah to transfer out of my department."

Carmella's eyes widened. "What?"

Matt coolly said, "We tried a personal relationship. It didn't work."

"So now you want her out?" Carmella gasped.

"It's not that simple."

"Then explain it to me."

"Actually, Carmella," Matt said angrily, "I don't think this is any of your business."

Carmella sucked in a breath. Sarah held hers. No one spoke to Lloyd's assistant in that tone or in that way. Not because Carmella had Lloyd's ear, but because Carmella was a sweet woman who wouldn't hurt a fly.

"I'm sorry," Matt immediately apologized, restoring Sarah's faith in his basic goodness. "I didn't mean that the way it sounded. But it isn't really any of your concern and it is something that's hard for me to talk about."

With that he walked into his office and closed the door. Sarah blinked back tears.

"This hurts him as much as it hurts you," Carmella observed softly.

"Yeah."

"So what happened?"

Sarah raised her gaze to meet Carmella's. "Mary Jane paid him a visit to warn him about his gold-digger assistant."

Carmella sucked in her breath again.

"She even offered to help Matt get me to back off. And it would only cost him a mere ten thousand dollars a visit."

"Oh, my God!"

"She also hit him up for fifty thousand dollars."

Carmella's wide eyes got even wider. "For what?"

"Apparently, she wants payment for having gone through pregnancy, labor and delivery."

"I am so sorry, Sarah. We really botched this."

"Actually, Carmella, *we* didn't. *I* did." Sarah paused, considered that, then added, "I take that back. Technically I didn't 'botch' anything. I'm just myself. Matt thinks we're opposites. My interference in his private life seemed to prove it to him."

"So he isn't rejecting you because we talked to his mother?"

"No, he's rejecting me because I'm me."

At that Sarah's eyes filled with tears and Carmella put her arm around her shoulders. "There's nothing wrong with you, Sarah."

"I know."

"Out there somewhere there's a man who is going to adore your feistiness and sense of adventure."

"I know. But it just seems wrong that it can't be the man I want it to be."

"Sometimes life sucks."

When Carmella used the off-color phrase, Sarah

laughed. "You better get back to work before Lloyd comes looking for you."

"Yeah," Carmella said, then stepped away. "Just remember to keep your chin up."

"I will."

"Maybe your secret admirer will send you something else?"

"Yeah, that would be peachy. Then I could get a hundred visitors and Matt could get even angrier with me."

"At least no one would question why you were transferring out."

Sarah laughed. "Right. That's exactly the excuse I used with Nelson this morning. I told him Matt kept getting perturbed about the crowds I drew with my secret admirer gifts."

"Works for me!" Carmella said.

Smiling bravely, Sarah said, "I'm hoping it works for everyone."

When the candy arrived at ten-thirty, Sarah's eyes filled with tears. Not because she was upset by the gift, but because she suspected Nelson had sent it, if only to help her carry out her charade.

Once again, her desk was surrounded by curiosity seekers. Only this time their number had grown. Suspiciously absent was Nelson.

Sarah cleared her throat, and reached for the little envelope to pull out the card. "It says, 'I will reveal...'" She paused. This was a real message. Silently she read the words on the card. *I will reveal myself at the charity ball tonight.* The note stunned her and was not something she intended for everyone to hear until she'd had a chance to digest it herself.

She looked up at the eager faces of the people surrounding her desk, cleared her throat again and, pretending to be reading, said, "I will reveal my love with this box of candy."

"There's that word *love* again," Sunny said with a laugh. "I think this guy is really serious, Sarah."

"Me, too," Ariana said.

"And I think you guys are going to get Sarah in trouble again!" Nelson said from the back of the crowd. "Get back to your desks."

"Yes," Carmella seconded, walking down the hall. "This has gone on long enough. Matt hasn't been happy with these gatherings from the beginning. Neither has Mr. Winters. I think it's shortsighted of you all not to notice that you're getting Sarah in trouble."

A general grumble rose from the crowd but they dispersed. Practicing what he preached, Nelson led the way.

Carmella walked up to Sarah's desk. "Are you okay?"

She nodded and wordlessly handed Carmella the card. She read it and her mouth fell open slightly. "Oh, my!" She peeked up at Sarah. "What are you going to do?"

For a few seconds Sarah considered that. She was losing her job and she had lost the love of her life because of the person sending her all this stuff. If it was Nelson, part of her wanted to meet with him, just for the chance to tell him that his gestures, kind as they seemed, had cost her much more than she wanted to lose.

Of course, getting her away from Matt might have been Nelson's purpose all along. And she had to wonder if that was such a bad purpose. Not just because Nelson might want her for himself, but also because he might have seen from the beginning that she and Matt weren't right for each other. The truth was, even their short attempt at a relationship had ended in disaster. Maybe Nelson had seen the handwriting on the wall all along...

And if he was that smart, maybe he was somebody worth meeting.

"I have to be at the charity ball anyway. So I might as well make myself available to anybody who wants to announce himself."

Carmella took a pace back. "You can't be serious."

Sarah lifted her chin. "I am. This guy has sent me something every time when I needed it. The first flowers came when I was down. The second flowers came when I was reconsidering my makeover. The candy came when I was upset. This candy and the notice that he was ready to meet me came right when I'm ready to meet him." She caught Carmella's gaze. "Whoever this guy is, he knows me. He *likes* me." She patted her chest. "He likes *me.*"

"Sarah, you're upset because of Matt. And I think you're reading too much into this."

Sarah shook her head. "I don't. I think what I am is ready. Ready to meet a new person. Ready to get on with the rest of my life...without Matt."

Carmella blew her breath out on a long, uncertain sigh. "All right. But don't go it alone. Rally the troops. Make enough people aware of what's going on that just in case it's not Nelson, you don't find yourself in a bad situation."

Matt heard the commotion at Sarah's desk and knew another secret admirer gift had arrived. The usual burst of jealousy spiraled through him. But this time he stopped it. He meant what he had said the night before. He and Sarah were not a good match. Polar opposites did nothing but drive each other crazy. As much as it hurt to let her go, he had to do it.

And that meant he couldn't be jealous.

But that didn't stop him from sneaking out to her desk when she left with Carmella for lunch. He opened her desk drawer, found the candy and slid the note from its envelope.

The secret admirer intended to reveal himself that night? At the ball?

This time the burst Matt got wasn't jealousy but protectiveness. God only knew who this man was. And since the charity ball was an event Lloyd hosted to raise funds, it was open to the public. Anybody with two hundred dollars could attend. And Sarah's guy had already proved he had money.

Fear caused Matt's throat to tighten, and he decided that he had to protect her. But as quickly as he had that thought he remembered what she'd told him when he'd accused her of interfering in the situation with his mother. She'd accused him of meddling in her life, too.

And he had. He hadn't seen it before. He'd seen himself as looking out for Sarah, but when he held his behavior against Sarah visiting his mother, he had to admit there was little difference.

He tapped the card against his palm. Sarah was smart, savvy and able to hold her own with ranch hands. There was no reason for Matt to worry about her in a roomful of people.

He thought of her dancing in the arms of another man and his chest tightened. He'd never wanted a woman the way he wanted her.

But he couldn't have her. And her secret admirer might actually be a wonderful guy.

He slid the card back into the envelope and closed her desk drawer, feeling very much as if he had closed the door on their relationship.

He was going to let her go.

Chapter Eleven

"What are you doing here?" Matt's dad asked as Matt walked into the foyer of his home. "I thought you were going to that fancy charity ball tonight?"

"I changed my mind."

"But you rented a tux!" Wayne said, leading his son to his kitchen, where dinner awaited. "And I wasn't expecting you for dinner. I only made spaghetti and meatballs."

"I'm actually in the mood for something simple."

Wayne stopped by the swinging door that led into the kitchen. "Oh-oh."

"Don't oh-oh me as if you know there's something wrong."

"There's definitely something wrong. You've changed your mind about going to the charity ball your company sponsors, in spite of the fact that you know Lloyd Winters will probably call you on the carpet Monday for not going."

"I'll make a healthy donation."

"Yeah, that might get you out of that end of the deal, but it doesn't change the fact that you're looking forward to spaghetti. I know there's something wrong, so just spill it."

Matt sighed heavily. It wasn't that he wanted to keep this from his dad. It wasn't even that he thought he *could* keep this from his dad. The fact was, losing Sarah wasn't easy for him to talk about.

Still, he knew his dad would badger him until he talked, so he chose to take the less-complicated track.

"Sarah asked for a transfer out of my department today."

"Oh, geez, I'm sorry," Wayne immediately apologized and so contritely that Matt nearly groaned. "I know how much you liked her work. It's gonna hurt like hell to lose her. Particularly since year-end is coming around. What was she thinking?"

Matt sighed. Leave it to his dad to figure out the perfect thing to say to force him to tell the whole story. "Having you apologize and assume Sarah is at fault makes me feel really great, Dad, like I'm the Grinch, or Scrooge."

"*You* did something that made her want to transfer out?"

"I *asked* her to transfer out."

Wayne shook his head and walked past the table to the stove. He lifted the pot of spaghetti and set it on the table. "Matt, I can't keep up with you."

"Lately, I can't keep up with myself."

"All right, let's start with the obvious question," Wayne said, as he helped himself to a healthy portion of pasta. "Why did you ask her to transfer out?"

"Because she went to see Mom."

Wayne's pasta stopped midway to his plate. "What?"

"She went to see Mom, and because she did, Mom came to see me."

"To ask for money," Wayne speculated dully, obviously knowing what had happened without even hearing the story.

"To *demand* money. She wanted fifty thousand dollars."

"And if you had given it to her she would have been back for fifty thousand more next month."

"I know."

Wayne sighed. "I know you do. You're a smart man, but you were an even brighter boy. You didn't jump to conclusions or get mad at me or your mom when we divorced. You understood that I didn't lie when I said your mom and I split because I didn't make enough money. But you also read between the lines. There was always food on our table. Our bills were paid. But your mother wanted more than I could provide."

"And you let me make up my own mind."

Wayne caught Matt's gaze. "It was the fair thing to do."

Matt nodded. "I appreciate that."

"So, why did Sarah go to see your mom?"

"She had this stupid notion that I couldn't commit to her because I was trapped by my past."

"Were you?"

Matt emphatically shook his head. "No!"

"Then why couldn't you commit?"

"Because we're opposites!"

"I don't think you are."

"You obviously didn't spend enough time with us then."

"I spent plenty of time with you. I saw you together at two parties and I saw you together at work twice."

Matt rolled his eyes. "Like that's really enough time to make an informed opinion."

Wayne laughed. "It was plenty of time. I saw that she made cow eyes at you and that you were solicitous."

"It's the proper thing to do."

"I never saw you worrying about any of the other ladies from your office. You never ran to get *them* drinks or find *them* seats."

Matt sighed.

Wayne quieted his voice. "Look, Matt, Sarah's a sweet, sincere woman."

"Who went to see my mother!"

"So?"

"So?" Matt asked incredulously. "She butted into my life!"

"From the few tidbits you mentioned to me over the past few weeks you did the same thing when you kept calling her secret admirer a stalker."

"He could be a stalker," Matt reminded his dad. "But you're right. I didn't have any right to butt into her life about that. And she didn't have any right to butt into mine."

Wayne shook his head. "Don't you see? The reason you and Sarah butt into each other's lives is because you're both desperate for an avenue to get in."

"That's crazy."

"That's human nature. You're both looking for a way in because there is no clear path because you are so different."

Matt stared at his dad for a second, then he chuckled. "Dad, you just made my argument."

"No, I didn't. You like each other. You want to be together but you're like two bulls in a china shop in each other's lives."

"Dad, we don't fit. I'm conservative. She's wacky. Silly. Funny. Off the wall."

"Which, Matt, is probably what you need in your extremely dull life. You don't want someone exactly like you or you'd be bored to death."

"My life isn't dull…"

The ringing of Matt's cell phone stopped him. He pulled it out of his jacket pocket and recognized Carmella's office number on caller ID.

Knowing she would only call in a crisis, he hit the button and said, "Hey, what's up?"

"Oh, Matt!" Carmella said, obviously upset. "The worst thing has happened."

Fear tightened Matt's throat. "With Lloyd? Is he okay? He's not sick, is he?"

"No, he's fine. It's Sarah."

Fear for Lloyd was bad enough. Fear for Sarah was instinctively paralyzing. Matt's heart froze in his chest. "Sarah? Has she been in an accident?"

"No, but she's about to have the worst night of her life."

Having endured a near heart attack for something he considered frivolous, Matt almost closed his cell phone. Worse, he was beginning to see that just like the secret admirer, Carmella was always in the right place at the right time to nudge him and Sarah in the direction of romance. And all she had accomplished was to get both of them hurt and leave them bewildered.

"I can't help you with that Carmella."

"You have to, Matt! She got candy today. The card said her secret admirer would be at the ball tonight."

It hurt to think of Sarah with another man, and Matt knew he was as tense about this as Carmella appeared to be, but he also knew he had no right to interfere. He had to let her go. No matter how much it hurt. "I know."

"Well, he isn't going."

The tone of Carmella's voice confirmed Matt's suspicions. Carmella was the one sending the flowers and candy. "I see. You sent her the candy today, thinking you would make me jealous and that I would change my mind about our relationship."

There was a long pause at the other end of the line. Finally, Carmella said, "What?"

"You're the secret admirer but your candy didn't work today. You didn't change my mind…"

"Matt, I don't understand half of what you're saying, but I don't have time to argue. Nelson got promoted this afternoon. He's becoming head of troubleshooting in Europe."

Matt stared at his phone, thinking he must have a bad connection or heard wrong. "What does Nelson have to do with anything?"

"Sarah said she thought Nelson had sent the candy today. Even if he didn't send the other gifts, he sent today's, which means he was the guy who was going to show up to declare his love tonight."

"Oh."

"When Lloyd told Nelson of his promotion, he handed him a ticket to Paris and instructed him to go apartment-hunting this weekend."

"Oh." Matt squeezed his eyes shut. "So he's not going to the ball."

"No, he's not." Carmella paused a second, then

softly said, "Matt, she's going to be very embarrassed."

Matt swallowed and the tightness in his chest increased a hundredfold. Not because he was jealous, but because he was furious. He couldn't believe someone could be so thoughtless as to hurt Sarah this way. He would choke Nelson if he got his hands on him.

"Matt, I can't tell you what to do, but you have to do something."

"Can't you call her and tell her what you just told me?"

"Nelson's promotion is a secret except to upper management."

"Can't you generically warn her that her secret admirer isn't going to show?"

"There's an entire party of friends going to the ball to support her. If I arrive and tell her that no one is coming, even if she sneaks out the back door, she's got to face everybody Monday morning."

Matt groaned and said, "Carmella, the only thing I could do to save her is pretend to be the secret admirer."

"Couldn't you?"

In his head, Matt tried to run through the consequences of doing something so foolish, but his thoughts were clouded by his feelings for Sarah and anger at Nelson, and he couldn't seem to draw a logical conclusion.

"I'll think about it."

"Please," Carmella said.

"Carmella, the consequences to this could be as bad for Sarah as having no secret admirer show up."

Carmella sighed. "I know, but…"

"Just let me think about it," Matt said and hung up his phone.

"Who was that?" his father asked.

"Carmella. Lloyd's assistant."

"And?"

"And Sarah's secret admirer isn't going to show up tonight."

"So there really is one?"

"Well, I'm not sure. Carmella could have sent the original flowers, playing matchmaker, and Nelson could have picked up the ball because he also had a crush on Sarah."

"So why isn't he coming tonight?"

"Because he got promoted. He's going to Paris apartment-hunting."

"And Sarah's going to be standing on the sidelines all night, dressed in something pretty, waiting for somebody who isn't going to show up."

"That's about the size of it," Matt said bouncing from his chair to pace. "I could punch that guy! He's so engrossed in software that he never thinks anything through and he's going to hurt her!"

But Wayne laughed. "Look at you! Instead of being worried that you were almost upstaged by a computer nerd, you're ready to sock the guy as if he were real competition. You're all but foaming at the mouth. You like this girl so much you're ready to fight for her."

"But we're not right for each other!"

"Make yourself right for each other!" When Matt said nothing, his father gentled his tone. "Matt, you need her. The thing I never told you about your mother and me was that she and I were exactly alike. I understood why she left without a backward glance because we were two peas in a pod. Being forced to raise you by myself made me slow down and that was when I realized why Mary Jane and I couldn't have made it. We were too much alike.''

Matt glanced over at his dad, but he said nothing.

Wayne continued, "You don't want to marry somebody just like you. You want to take the risk with your opposite because you're not only going to be forced to grow, to become more than you could ever be by yourself, but you're also going to have a fun, exciting time together. You remember good times, don't you?''

"Very funny, Dad.''

"No, it's not funny. You've worked too hard all your life. It's time to slow down a bit.'' Wayne paused and smiled. "Did you ever stop to think that the reason you're so attracted to Sarah is that deep down inside you already know all this? Deep down inside you're ready for some fun?''

Matt arrived at the hotel about a half hour after the festivities had started. Dressed in his tux and furious with Nelson O'Connor, he jogged through the lobby and to the ballroom.

He glanced around the room once and only once before he saw Sarah. Wearing a formfitting red gown, with her hair spilling around her, she was the most beautiful woman in the room.

Unfortunately, she was standing in a huddle of Wintersoft employees. Not only were Ariana and Sunny by her side, but Grant Lawson and Jack Devon stood just slightly to their right. Reed Connors, Nate Leeman and Brett Hamilton were in a conversation group to her left.

Matt knew the women were there to support Sarah, but he guessed the men hung back, within hearing distance, only partly from curiosity. From the set of their shoulders, Matt recognized they were standing there for the very same reason Matt would be if he hadn't been so obstinate. To protect her.

Carmella was right. Everybody Sarah worked with was in some way, shape or form, involved in this. If a secret admirer didn't show, Sarah would be embarrassed mightily.

He drew a long breath to gather his courage and walked over. "Hi, can I have this dance?" he asked, taking Sarah's champagne glass from her hand and giving it to Ariana.

Clearly not happy with Matt, Ariana frowned as she took the champagne Matt shoved at her. "What are you doing here?" she asked defensively, obviously knowing about the disagreement he and Sarah had had.

"I'm…" he began, but Emily interrupted him from behind.

"Yeah, Matt. What are you doing here?"

He turned to face the woman he was sure would someday be his boss and almost answered, but he stopped dead in his tracks. Not only had the five men in the two clusters off to the side of Sarah focused their attention completely on him, but the man who had his arm wrapped around Emily's shoulders looked like something out of… Well, out of a Broadway musical.

"Good evening, Emily," Matt said, not quite sure what else to say. He was so stunned by her date's perfectly coifed hair and expensive-looking diamond earring that he temporarily forgot all about Sarah.

Jack Devon seemed to have the same reaction to Emily's date that Matt did.

"Hi, Emily," Jack said, strolling over. Dressed in a black tuxedo, Jack looked like every other man in the room, except Jack always had a glint of something secret in his eyes. Matt didn't know what it was, because he didn't make it his business to poke in the affairs of other people—especially not men who didn't care to talk about their pasts. But if he were a betting man, he would take the wager that Carmella would get the story out of Jack one day.

"Who's your friend?" Jack asked with an obvious hint of amusement.

"Steven Hansen," Emily replied a little too coolly, Matt thought.

"Steven," Matt said, extending his hand to shake Emily's date's hand, trying to diffuse the sudden chill in the air. "It's nice to meet you."

"Nice to meet you, too, Matt," Steven replied, then shook hands with all the employees as Emily introduced them.

Though every person in the group of Wintersoft employees appeared to quickly assess the situation with Emily's date and recognize the farce, Matt noted that her dad did not.

"Steven," Lloyd said, slapping the ornately dressed man on the back as he joined the conversation group. "Having a good time?"

"The best, sir," Steven replied and Matt suddenly saw the ruse for what it was. Her date was clearly gay, but it seemed Emily wasn't trying to fool anybody but her dad into thinking that she had a boyfriend, and it appeared for the time being she had succeeded.

"So, Matt, what brings you here?" Lloyd asked, looking Matt in the eye. "I seem to recall a voice-mail message in which you begged off having to attend. I also recall a two-thousand-dollar donation as penance. I hope your being here doesn't mean you think you can rescind that offer."

"No, sir, I don't," Matt said, stealing a quick glance at Sarah who looked to be ready to slip away from the group. He caught her hand and stopped her. "I'm actually here to see Sarah. So I still intend to make the donation. But," he added glancing around at the curious faces. "You're all going to have to excuse us for a few seconds. At least long enough for one dance."

With that he tugged on Sarah's hand and dragged her out onto the dance floor.

"What the heck do you think you're doing?"

"Saving you."

"Saving me?"

"Yes, Nelson's not coming."

She stiffened in his arms and pushed back slightly. "He's not?"

"No."

Her eyes narrowed. "How do you know?"

"Because Carmella called me. She would have told you herself, but as you can see," Matt said, directing Sarah's attention to Lloyd Winters who was back to mingling with the crowd of donors, keeping his assistant busy by his side as he did so, "She can't get away from Lloyd. It's an important night for him."

"I see."

Recognizing how difficult this was for Sarah, Matt drew a long breath. "I'm sorry."

"Right."

"No, I am. I know how you felt about having a secret admirer. I know you probably would have given Nelson a real chance. If only because he was so romantic."

"He *is* romantic." She paused and glanced at Matt. "So where is he?"

Matt drew a quick breath. "I'm going to tell you, but first you have to promise to keep it a secret."

"A secret?"

"Yes. As confidential as anything I tell you as your boss. Promise?"

She nodded. "I promise."

"He's being transferred to Paris."

Sarah's eyes widened. "Holy cow!"

"Lloyd gave him tickets to fly over and apartment-hunt this weekend."

"Wow."

"So that means the possibility exists that he'll be back on Tuesday or so, offering you a chance to move to Paris."

Sarah pressed her hand to her chest. "Holy hell."

Matt laughed. "I see my old Sarah is back."

"Get used to it because I like the real me. No more changes not even for you."

"That's good because I always liked the old Sarah, too. But that also means you've got one heck of a decision to make. And I'm going to add something else to the mix that's going to make it even harder."

"I can't see how."

"I'm going to ask you not to go to Paris with Nelson. I want you to stay in Boston."

Sarah stopped dancing. "Why?"

Matt licked his suddenly dry lips. "I don't want to work with you anymore. That only complicates things."

Sarah took a pace back out of his arms. "So, you've told me. And since I do nothing but complicate your life, I would think you would be thrilled if I moved to Paris."

She turned away, but Matt grabbed her hand and forced her to face him again. He caught the gaze of her beautiful green eyes and held it. "I would miss you."

"Yeah, like how you'll miss me when I leave your department."

"I'll miss you a lot."

"Right."

"I will! I'm sorry I asked you to transfer. I know I said and did some really stupid things."

"I've got news for you, Matt. You said and did your most stupid things long before you forced me to transfer out of your department."

"Because I was scared."

"Right."

"I was. I didn't want to end up like my parents. So I spent my entire life doing everything in my power to make sure I was ready for marriage and looking for potential ways relationships could fail. Turns out, the whole thing was out of my hands anyway."

"Matt, I'm starting to think you need therapy." With a sigh she pivoted and began walking away.

"Sarah, don't! The thing I hated about us, that we're opposites, is the thing that attracts me to you. I need you in my life. I need your humor and warmth and love of life."

Sarah stared at him.

"The truth is, I've been falling in love with you since the day we met, Sarah. You can't leave me now."

He pulled a diamond engagement ring out of his pocket. "So, I'm asking you to marry me before Nelson gets home. I know it's not fair. I believe it might actually be cheating. I don't care. I don't intend to lose you."

Sarah stared at him. "What about Nelson?"

Matt took a step forward. "You don't love Nelson."

"No, I don't."

"Yet you were willing to give him a chance. You

were willing to be open-minded and flexible and give him lots of room to make mistakes while you fell in love with him.''

She swallowed.

''You're going to need that with me.''

She shook her head. ''No. I won't. I already love you.''

''Then take the ring,'' Matt said and slipped it on her finger. ''I love you more than anything. Half the reason I wouldn't get involved with you was that I didn't want to hurt you. Now, I know I won't.''

Sarah glanced up at him, her eyes filled with tears. ''No, you won't. Or you won't just answer to my daddy, you'll answer to the fifty ranch hands who attend the ceremony, one rich socialite mother...'' she held his gaze. ''And me.''

At that, Matt laughed. ''I have a sneaky feeling you're going to have to teach me how to ride.''

''And rope and spend the night on the range.''

Matt laughed. ''My life is never going to be dull again.''

Sarah smiled. ''No. It isn't. I promise.''

Epilogue

Carmella heard Emily's date, Steve Hansen, excuse himself just as Lloyd got involved in a serious discussion about interest rates. So, she slipped away, over to Emily, who stood off to the right of the dance floor, wide-eyed and gasping for breath.

"Did you see that?" Emily asked Carmella. "Matt just put a ring on Sarah's finger!"

"I know!" Carmella said, almost singing for joy.

"They're engaged!" Emily grinned. "We didn't do a darned thing and one of our bachelors is down."

Carmella laughed. "I wouldn't say we didn't do anything. We more than helped her with her makeover and I was constantly giving them advice. Plus, you sent the first roses."

Emily shook her head. "I didn't send those roses. I thought you did."

"My Lord!" Carmella gasped. "Maybe it really was Nelson!"

Emily laughed. "Doesn't matter. Not only did Nelson

get a big enough promotion to make him forget all about his crush on Sarah, but he's also moving to Paris. City of love. He'll easily find a replacement. Look at them,'' she said, pointing to happy Sarah and Matt who were showing off her engagement ring to their coworkers. "They're so darned happy!''

"Yes, they are,'' Carmella agreed. But she couldn't help but notice there were still five Wintersoft bachelors in the group of people clustered around the newly engaged couple. Tall, good-looking Reed Connors. Gorgeous, blue-eyed Grant Lawson. Brett Hamilton, the sandy-haired Brit who carried himself like royalty. And even serious senior Vice President of Technology Nate Leeman, who was every bit as handsome as the other senior VPs when dressed in his tuxedo.

Because of their jobs at Wintersoft, those four all had good careers and solid futures. Most of them would end up wealthy. Plus, they were good-looking and eligible. Carmella knew Lloyd considered all of them son-in-law material. Even Jack Devon, the elusive man of mystery, would make Lloyd's list if only because Lloyd loved him like a son.

Wintersoft, Inc., was a haven of potential sons-in-law, and Emily Winters was not out of the woods yet.

* * * * *

*Turn the page for a sneak preview
of the next*
MARRYING THE BOSS'S DAUGHTER
*title
featuring Grant and Ariana's story:*
HER PREGNANT AGENDA
*by Linda Goodnight
on sale October 2003 (SR #1690).*

Chapter One

"Ariana," Grant said gently. "Sooner or later, your family will have to be told. You can't keep two babies a secret forever."

"I know." She pulled in a ragged sigh. "I know. In fact, I really meant to all along, but first I wanted to get married—Mama's old-fashioned about that. I'd told the entire family about the engagement, but Benjy was always vague about the wedding date, not making a commitment until three days before the courthouse fiasco. I'd planned to let them know about the babies once we married. When that never happened and I had to tell them about the breakup, I couldn't bring myself to reveal the pregnancy at the same time. One shock was enough. But the longer I put off telling them, the harder it became."

"Procrastination's hell." He should know. Hadn't he said he'd "think about" that high-profile position with his dad's law firm instead of refusing straight off the way he'd wanted to?

"No kidding. But once the babies come and I have my life under control again, everything will be fine and I'll announce them to the world. Oh, Grant, I love these babies so much. My soul sings every time I think of watching them grow from perfect babies into beautiful, unique individuals. I can't wait to hold them and count their fingers and kiss their noses and—" One nail-chewed hand flew to her mouth. "I'm sorry. You didn't ask for all that motherly gushing."

Some odd emotion caught in his chest at Ariana's passionate speech. He'd dreamed of seeing that expression on Tiffany's face, of sharing the unbridled joy of pregnancy and childbirth with the woman he loved. But Tiffany had put an end to such foolish fantasies.

Carefully, deliberately, he shifted his attention back to a woman who did want children. As an attorney he empathized to a certain point with all his clients, but Ariana didn't appear to want his sympathy. Though she'd made some mistakes, she didn't wallow in self-pity, and, unlike her ex-fiancé, Ariana took full responsibility for her life, embracing the good parts of a difficult situation. He admired that. Yes, that was it. He admired her grit and determination. And he'd darn well find a way to see her through this difficult period.

He was still contemplating the particulars of such action, when the rotund waiter approached the table. "Sir, would you and the wife care for some dessert?"

Not wanting to embarrass the waiter, Grant ignored the mistake and shook his head. "None for me. Ariana?"

"No, thank you." He could see that she was disconcerted by the waiter's presumption that they were married. She dipped her head and fiddled with the remaining linguini, a pose he found both lovely and alluring.

Long, dark eyelashes curved over the crests of her delicate, pink-tinged cheekbones.

For a moment he let his mind slide into the thought planted by the hapless waiter and the memories of Tiffany's cruelty. What if Ariana were his wife? What if those were his babies she carried beneath her heart? Regardless of Tiffany's taunts, he'd yearned to be a father, a good one. To take his children to the Cape and teach them to sail. Or to deep-sea fish and dig clams. Ariana would look beautiful walking barefoot along a sun-kissed beach with her rich, dark hair blowing in the breeze.

"Your check, sir." The waiter's voice pulled him out of his reverie. Swallowing thickly, he forced his gaze away from Ariana's lovely profile and reached for his wallet.

Teeth clenched, he reminded himself that the case against marriage was settled long ago. As much as the truth pained him, there would be no children for Grant Lawson. And certainly no wife. Never, never, never a wife.

*   *   *   *   *

If you enjoyed what you just read,
then we've got an offer you can't resist!

Take 2 bestselling
love stories FREE!
Plus get a FREE surprise gift!

Clip this page and mail it to Silhouette Reader Service™

IN U.S.A.
3010 Walden Ave.
P.O. Box 1867
Buffalo, N.Y. 14240-1867

IN CANADA
P.O. Box 609
Fort Erie, Ontario
L2A 5X3

YES! Please send me 2 free Silhouette Romance® novels and my free surprise gift. After receiving them, if I don't wish to receive anymore, I can return the shipping statement marked cancel. If I don't cancel, I will receive 6 brand-new novels every month, before they're available in stores! In the U.S.A., bill me at the bargain price of $3.34 plus 25¢ shipping and handling per book and applicable sales tax, if any*. In Canada, bill me at the bargain price of $3.80 plus 25¢ shipping and handling per book and applicable taxes**. That's the complete price and a savings of at least 10% off the cover prices—what a great deal! I understand that accepting the 2 free books and gift places me under no obligation ever to buy any books. I can always return a shipment and cancel at any time. Even if I never buy another book from Silhouette, the 2 free books and gift are mine to keep forever.

215 SDN DNUM
315 SDN DNUN

Name	(PLEASE PRINT)	
Address	Apt.#	
City	State/Prov.	Zip/Postal Code

 * Terms and prices subject to change without notice. Sales tax applicable in N.Y.
** Canadian residents will be charged applicable provincial taxes and GST.
   All orders subject to approval. Offer limited to one per household and not valid to
   current Silhouette Romance® subscribers.
   ® are registered trademarks of Harlequin Books S.A., used under license.

SROM02   ©1998 Harlequin Enterprises Limited

Your opinion is important to us! Please take a few moments to share your thoughts with us about your experiences with Harlequin and Silhouette books. Your comments will be very useful in ensuring that we deliver books you love to read. ***Please take a few minutes to complete the questionnaire, then send it to us at the address below.***

Send your completed questionnaires to:
Harlequin/Silhouette Reader Survey, P.O. Box 9046, Buffalo, NY 14269-9046

1. As you may know, there are many different lines under the Harlequin and Silhouette brands. Each of the lines is listed below. Please check the box that most represents your reading habit for each line.

Line	Currently read this line	Do not read this line	Not sure if I read this line
Harlequin American Romance	❑	❑	❑
Harlequin Duets	❑	❑	❑
Harlequin Romance	❑	❑	❑
Harlequin Historicals	❑	❑	❑
Harlequin Superromance	❑	❑	❑
Harlequin Intrigue	❑	❑	❑
Harlequin Presents	❑	❑	❑
Harlequin Temptation	❑	❑	❑
Harlequin Blaze	❑	❑	❑
Silhouette Special Edition	❑	❑	❑
Silhouette Romance	❑	❑	❑
Silhouette Intimate Moments	❑	❑	❑
Silhouette Desire	❑	❑	❑

2. Which of the following best describes why you bought *this book*? One answer only, please.

the picture on the cover	❑	the title	❑
the author	❑	the line is one I read often	❑
part of a miniseries	❑	saw an ad in another book	❑
saw an ad in a magazine/newsletter	❑	a friend told me about it	❑
I borrowed/was given this book	❑	other: _____	❑

3. Where did you buy *this book*? One answer only, please.

at Barnes & Noble	❑	at a grocery store	❑
at Waldenbooks	❑	at a drugstore	❑
at Borders	❑	on eHarlequin.com Web site	❑
at another bookstore	❑	from another Web site	❑
at Wal-Mart	❑	Harlequin/Silhouette Reader	❑
at Target	❑	Service/through the mail	
at Kmart	❑	used books from anywhere	❑
at another department store or mass merchandiser	❑	I borrowed/was given this book	❑

4. On average, how many Harlequin and Silhouette books do you buy at one time?

I buy _____ books at one time ❑
I rarely buy a book ❑

MRQ403SR-1A

5. How many times per month do you shop for any *Harlequin and/or Silhouette* books?
One answer only, please.

1 or more times a week	❑	a few times per year	❑
1 to 3 times per month	❑	less often than once a year	❑
1 to 2 times every 3 months	❑	never	❑

6. When you think of your ideal heroine, which *one* statement describes her the best?
One answer only, please.

She's a woman who is strong-willed	❑	She's a desirable woman	❑
She's a woman who is needed by others	❑	She's a powerful woman	❑
She's a woman who is taken care of	❑	She's a passionate woman	❑
She's an adventurous woman	❑	She's a sensitive woman	❑

7. The following statements describe types or genres of books that you may be
interested in reading. Pick *up to 2 types* of books that you are most interested in.

I like to read about truly romantic relationships ❑
I like to read stories that are sexy romances ❑
I like to read romantic comedies ❑
I like to read a romantic mystery/suspense ❑
I like to read about romantic adventures ❑
I like to read romance stories that involve family ❑
I like to read about a romance in times or places that I have never seen ❑
Other: _____ ❑

*The following questions help us to group your answers with those readers who are
similar to you. Your answers will remain confidential.*

8. Please record your year of birth below.
19 ____

9. What is your marital status?
single ❑   married ❑   common-law ❑   widowed ❑
divorced/separated ❑

10. Do you have children 18 years of age or younger currently living at home?
yes ❑   no ❑

11. Which of the following best describes your employment status?
employed full-time or part-time ❑   homemaker ❑   student ❑
retired ❑   unemployed ❑

12. Do you have access to the Internet from either home or work?
yes ❑   no ❑

13. Have you ever visited eHarlequin.com?
yes ❑   no ❑

14. What state do you live in?
_____

15. Are you a member of Harlequin/Silhouette Reader Service?
yes ❑   Account # _____   no ❑   MRQ403SR-1B

SILHOUETTE *Romance*

COMING NEXT MONTH

#1690 HER PREGNANT AGENDA—Linda Goodnight
Marrying the Boss's Daughter
General Counsel Grant Lawson agreed to protect
Ariana Fitzpatrick—and her unborn twins—from her custody-
seeking, two-timing ex-fiancé. But delivering the precious
babies and kissing their oh-so-beautiful mother senseless
weren't in his job description! And falling in love—well,
that *definitely* wasn't part of the agenda!

#1691 THE VISCOUNT & THE VIRGIN—Valerie Parv
The Carramer Trust
Legend claimed anyone who served the Merrisand Trust would
find true love, but the only thing Rowe Sevrin, Viscount Aragon,
found was feisty, fiery-haired temptress Kirsten Bond. How
could his reluctant assistant seem so innocent and inexperienced
and still be a mother? And why was her young son Rowe's spit-
ting image?

#1692 THE MOST ELIGIBLE DOCTOR
—Karen Rose Smith
Nurse Brianne Barrington had lost every person she'd ever
loved. So when she took the job with Jed Sawyer, a rugged,
capable doctor with emotional wounds of his own, she intended
to keep her distance. But Jed's tender embraces awakened a
womanly desire she'd never felt before. Could the cautious,
love-wary Brianna risk her heart again?

#1693 MARLIE'S MYSTERY MAN—Doris Rangel
Soulmates
Marlie Simms was falling for two men—sort of! One man
was romantic, sexy and funny, and the other was passionate,
determined and strong. Except they were *both* Caid Matthews—
a man whose car accident left his spirit split in two! And only
Marlie's love could make Caid a whole man again....